The Fighting Scouts by Edgar Wallace

Richard Horatio Edgar Wallace was born on the 1st April 1875 in Greenwich, London. Leaving school at 12 because of truancy, by the age of fifteen he had experience; selling newspapers, as a worker in a rubber factory, as a shoe shop assistant, as a milk delivery boy and as a ship's cook.

By 1894 he was engaged but broke it off to join the Infantry being posted to South Africa. He also changed his name to Edgar Wallace which he took from Lew Wallace, the author of *Ben-Hur*.

In Cape Town in 1898 he met Rudyard Kipling and was inspired to begin writing. His first collection of ballads, *The Mission that Failed!* was enough of a success that in 1899 he paid his way out of the armed forces in order to turn to writing full time.

By 1904 he had completed his first thriller, *The Four Just Men*. Since nobody would publish it he resorted to setting up his own publishing company which he called Tallis Press.

In 1911 his Congolese stories were published in a collection called *Sanders of the River*, which became a bestseller. He also started his own racing papers, *Bibury's* and *R. E. Walton's Weekly*, eventually buying his own racehorses and losing thousands gambling. A life of exceptionally high income was also mirrored with exceptionally large spending and debts.

Wallace now began to take his career as a fiction writer more seriously, signing with Hodder and Stoughton in 1921. He was marketed as the 'King of Thrillers' and they gave him the trademark image of a trilby, a cigarette holder and a yellow Rolls Royce. He was truly prolific, capable not only of producing a 70,000 word novel in three days but of doing three novels in a row in such a manner. It was estimated that by 1928 one in four books being read was written by Wallace, for alongside his famous thrillers he wrote variously in other genres, including science fiction, non-fiction accounts of WWI which amounted to ten volumes and screen plays. Eventually he would reach the remarkable total of 170 novels, 18 stage plays and 957 short stories.

Wallace became chairman of the Press Club which to this day holds an annual Edgar Wallace Award, rewarding 'excellence in writing'.

Diagnosed with diabetes his health deteriorated and he soon entered a coma and died of his condition and double pneumonia on the 7th of February 1932 in North Maple Drive, Beverly Hills. He was buried near his home in England at Chalklands, Bourne End, in Buckinghamshire.

Index of Contents

CHAPTER I

THE GENTLEMEN FROM INDIANA

Lieutenant Baxter was writing letters home and, at the moment Cornish came into the mess-hut, was gazing through the window with that fixed stare which might indicate either the memory of some one loved and absent or a mental struggle after the correct spelling of the village billets he had bombed the night before.

Cornish, who looked sixteen, but was in reality quite an old gentleman of twenty, thrust his hands into his breeches pockets and gazed disconsolately round before he slouched across to where Baxter sat at his literary exercises.

"I say," said Cornish in a complaining voice, "what the devil are you doing?"

"Cleaning my boots," said Baxter without looking up; "didn't you notice it?"

Second-Lieutenant Cornish sniggered. "Quit fooling. I say, what are you writing letters for? Good Heavens, you are always writing letters!"

Baxter withdrew his gaze from the window and went on writing with marked industry.

"I say," said Cornish again, "there was a fellow of the American squadron in here to-day."

Baxter sighed and put down his pen. "I am told that America is in the war," he said politely. "This fact would probably account for the phenomenal happening."

"He asked for rye whisky," said Cornish, nodding significantly.

"Poor fellow."

"When I told him that we hadn't any rye whisky," Cornish went on, "he asked, whether we weren't fighting for civilization and the free something or other of peoples."

Baxter swung round on his chair, his hands folded on his lap. "All this is very fascinating," he said; "why don't you write a book about it? And what are you doing here, may I ask? I thought you were going into Amiens?"

"I wish I'd gone," said the gloomy young man; "it is blowing eighty miles an hour up-stairs. Depledge went up and was buffeted about all over the shop and nearly crashed. Saw a Hun and couldn't get near him."

"What was the Hun doing?" asked Baxter, interested in spite of himself.

"That's the very question Depledge asked me."

"But you didn't tell him?" said Baxter. "You're a reticent devil, Cornish! And now, if you don't mind my communicating with my fond parents, perhaps you will go out into the garden and eat worms."

"Oh, that reminds me," said Cornish: "This American chap, a most excellent fellow, by the way, wanted to know what has happened to Tam."

"Did you tell him?"

"No," confessed Cornish.

"Do you know?" asked the patient Baxter.

"No," admitted Cornish.

Baxter groaned. "Good-by," he said.

"I say," said Cornish.

"Good-by," said Baxter loudly.

"This fellow," Cornish drawled on in his even, monotonous voice, "this American fellow. I mean, the American fellow I saw this morning—"

"I thought you were speaking about the Spanish fellow you saw yesterday," said Baxter wearily.

"No, this American fellow said that he had heard that Tam was coming back. Some brass-hat told him."

"He was pulling your leg, my dear Cornish," said Baxter; "these Americans stuff people, especially the young and the innocent. Now go to bed or go out and buy me some stamps or take my motor-bike and joy-ride into Amiens or go down to the workshop or—or go to the dickens."

"You are very unsociable," said Cornish, and wandered out.

He strolled across to the workshop and stood for a few minutes in that noisy hive watching the mechanics fitting a new tractor screw to his "camel," then walked back to his quarters through the drizzle.

The wind was blowing gustily. It slammed doors and sent gray clouds of smoke bellowing from the stove, it rattled the windows and whined and sobbed about the corners of the hut.

Then suddenly above the sigh and moan of it rose a shrill "whee-e-e!"

Cornish was in the act of sitting down as the sound came to him. He checked the action and, half-doubled as he was, leapt for the door and flung it open.

"Wh—oom—oom!"

The force of the explosion flung him back, the windows crashed outward, the ground beneath his feet rocked again.

Even as he fell he heard the shattering of wood where the bomb fragments ripped through the casings of the hut. He was on his feet in an instant and through the door.

High above the aerodrome, appearing and disappearing through the hurrying cloud-ruck, was a machine that swayed and jumped most visibly.

Cornish started at a run as the antiaircraft guns began their belated chorus.

He met Baxter struggling into his padded jacket before his hangar.

"We'll take a chance," said Baxter rapidly; "who'd ever imagine the swine would come over on a day like this?"

"Think he'll come back?" asked Cornish.

The other shouted something unintelligible as he turned to climb into his tiny one-seater and Cornish guessed rather than heard the answer.

Three minutes later he was zooming up behind his superior, his machine dancing like a scrap of paper caught in the wind. The little scout climbed steeply, heading eastward, and Cornish, strapped to his seat, saw nothing but the gray race of cloud above him, until the altimeter registered eight thousand feet. Then he began to take notice.

A little below him and a mile away was Baxter's machine, while a mile ahead of him and running across his bows was a Hun plane of respectable size and unusual lines. He observed with joy that the enemy was making bad weather of it, and banked round to run on a parallel course.

A rapid glimpse of the country told him that the adventurous enemy was making for home, and the proximity of the machine was probably due to the fact that the bomber had attempted to return against the wind to repeat his good work when he had sighted the chasers.

Baxter's scout swung round behind the enemy. Cornish closed to his flank. The astonished but interested infantry in the trenches eight thousand feet below, heard above the purr of the engines the "ral-tat-tat-tat-tat!" of machine guns and saw the Boche side-slip. It was a scientific side-slip, wholly designed as an advertisement of the slipper's distress, but it was not the weather for artful maneuvers. Suddenly the big machine began to spin, not a well-controlled spin, but rather following the motion of a corkscrew driven by a drunken hand.

The two scouts dived for him, their guns chattering excitedly, and the big Hun flip-flopped earthward, nose up, tail up, wing up—till he made a pancake crash midway between the line and the aerodrome of the Umpty-fourth.

Baxter followed and made a bad landing, but the Providence which protects the child was kinder to Cornish, who lit "like a blinking angel," to quote a muddy and unprejudiced representative of the P.B.I.*

[* The infantry is invariably referred to by all other arms as the "Poor Blooming Infantry." or words to that effect.—E.W.]

Luck was not wholly against the enemy (for the two German airmen were alive when their machine reached bottom) except that the friendly hands which had strapped them to their seats had done their work a little too effectively. By the time they had freed themselves from restraint, but before they had fired the incendiary bomb which was intended to destroy the machine, Baxter was out of his chaser and was standing on the under-carriage.

"Don't fire the machine unless you're awfully keen on a military funeral," he said, and four gloved hands arose over two leather-helmeted heads.

"Don't shoot. Colonel," said the cheerful pilot, "I'll come down."

Baxter watched his prisoners descend before he restored his Colt automatic to its holster.

"Sorry and all that sort of thing," he said to the pilot, "but you've got some nerve."

"Give the barbarian credit for something," replied the blue- eyed pilot, lighting a black cigar. "I'm afraid my friend here will want a doctor." He indicated the very young and very pale officer, whose thumb had apparently been shot away. "He doesn't speak English. My name is Prince Karl of Stettiz-Waldenstein, the last of the ancient race that carries the blood of Charlemagne."

"Cheerioh," said Baxter, "come along to our mess and have some lunch before the wolves get you and put you in a little cage. We'll drop your friend at the hospital—my name, by the way, is Baxter, and I come from a long line of hardware merchants."

The prince smiled. "Trade follows the flag," he said. "My little friend's father makes typewriters—and pretty bad ones. You ought to be friends."

An R.F.C. picked them up and after depositing the wounded youth at the general hospital, the two foemen were whirled back to the aerodrome, their arrival coinciding with the return of the majority of the squadron from Amiens. The prisoner was talkative and lively. He had been educated at Harvard and Oxford, thought the war was pretty good sport, told a joyous tale of a grand-ducal aunt who had sent him a set of silken underwear embarrassingly embroidered with the legend: "Gott strafe England und America," but would not offer any information about the machine he was flying.

"You can see what is left of it and discover for yourself," he said to Major Blackie at parting; "she's a fairly useful bus, but nothing as useful as she's supposed to be. Oh, by the way, I nearly forgot to ask—where's Tam?"

"Tam is in England," smiled Blackie. "I thought you fellows knew. He got married and went away to be an instructor or something."

"But surely he's back," persisted the other. "One of our circus commanders (you call them circuses, don't you?) told me he was due back to-day—that was one of the reasons I came over. If the weather had been good we should have come in force!"

"A sort of 'welcome home,' eh?"

The prince grinned.

"Well, he isn't here," Blackie went on, "and so far as I know—excuse me."

An orderly stood in the door with a scrap of paper in his hand which Blackie took and read.

"I must hurry you off," he said; "the wind's dropped and one of your circuses is going up."

"Good luck to 'em," said the prisoner as he shook hands.

The circus did not materialize in so far as the squadron was concerned, its activities being exclusively monopolized by certain enthusiastic but half-trained units of the U. S. F. C., which, while on a practise flight, and strictly against all instructions, engaged its more skilful enemy and bluffed it into retreat.

This was discussed among other matters after dinner that night.

"The gentlemen from Indiana got Fritz with his tail down," said Baxter; "they were out doing a formation stunt with no idea in life save to avoid unpleasantness with their flight commander—it wasn't a bad formation, by the way—when Fritz and his Imperial Circus butted into the simple children of the West."

"What happened?"

"It was funny. The gentlemen from Indiana just dropped that formation nonsense. They simply went baldheaded for the nearest Hun and before you could say 'knife,' two Huns were spinning out of control and the circus was moving homeward with the United States of America in hot pursuit. It was comic to see the French instructor shooting off frantic recall signals."

Blackie pulled out his cigar case and contemplated the interior with a look of gloom.

"I wonder why everybody thinks Tam is coming back—the cigars and the Americans remind me."

"I'll bet he's no use for flying—when a chap is married he's done for," said a voice in a dark corner.

"Hit him, somebody," growled Mortimer, the latest of the squadron benedicts. "Come out of your obscurity, Hector Misogynist; oh, it's Cornish! Bah!"

Cornish came into the light unabashed. "Kipling wrote it about a fellow who wouldn't take a fence or lead his squadron after he was married—got scared when he thought of his child and all that sort of thing."

The door opened suddenly and a muffled figure stood in the entrance.

"Waiting patrol!" he barked. "Get up—light, bombing squadron over Corps Headquarters—get a wiggle on!"

A scamper of feet, wails and imprecations from the waiting patrol, a chorus of "Shut that door—damn you!" and the hum of engines outside. A confusion of voices, a more intense roar which dies down to silence, and the night patrol is away.

Blackie looked at his watch. "Simmonds, your flight had better stand by—they don't usually strafe C. H. Q. There go our Archies—everybody stand by!"

Blackie hurried to his concrete office where a nonchalant telephonist was exchanging philosophy with another telephonist six miles away, and if the distant operator was the less philosophical of the two, he might be excused, since he was at that moment undergoing an aerial bombardment.

"Umpty-eighth bein' bombed, sir," reported the telephonist in the same surprised tone you might employ to announce that a football match had been postponed, "the 'Uns 'ave strafed two 'angars."

"And knocked the H's off the rest, eh?" said Blackie. "Ask O. Pip* if any of our people have signaled."

[* Observation post.]

Click! A plug pushed home, a rasping buzz and— "Hello—O. Pip—Hallow! O. Pip. Reports? Right." He turned. "Night squadron signaled nine thousand feet, sir—makin' west. Encountered no H.A."

He said this importantly, since there was a fine roll in "encountered" and a pleasant mystery—which was no mystery to anybody—in the abbreviations for "Hostile Aircraft" and "Observation Post."

Baxter came back ten minutes later to report and inquire. "They seem to be leaving us alone, which is strange, after what that prince person said."

"Apparently they are after the gentlemen from Indiana, who, I suppose, will be gnashing their teeth at their good kind instructor because he won't let them go up in the dark, dark night."

"We're a cheerful lot of boys," said Baxter. "Who called them the gentlemen from Indiana, by the way?"

"Tam," said Blackie laughing; "he'd read a book with a title like that—Indiana was the word that took Tam's fancy."

"Hello—hello—yes—speak up, Clarence—bombin' yer, are they—all right." The operator half turned. "Bombing Squadron H. A. operatin' over American Squadron H. Q., sir; one 'angar slightly damaged."

Blackie nodded.

"Hello! Yes—one H. A. forced to descend by Archie fire, sir."

Blackie nodded again. "They're out to-night with a vengeance," he said; "every bombing squadron Fritz has must be working."

"Headquarters call, sir," reported the telephonist and slipped the apparatus from his head.

Blackie sank into the seat vacated and adjusted the ear-pieces. "Yes—Umpty-fourth—yes, sir, Blackie speaking. Yes—they seem lively, yes, sir—(check this, Baxter) twelve machines to escort 947th and 958th squadrons on a bombing raid to be in the air at five aco-emma! (Got that, Baxter?) Yes, sir."

He hung up the receiver. "Reprisals by order—wind up at D.H.Q.—slow music and death to the sleep-destroying Hun!"

 With the dawn the escorting squadrons rose to their station, and Blackie from the ground saw the flicker of blue and green lights as the British bombing machines came over and their escort fell into place.

The drone of their engines had hushed to an intermittent buzz when Blackie strolled across the aerodrome to the deserted mess-room for his morning cup of tea.

The sergeant-major who walked at his side was expressing the gloomy views on the weather which sergeant-majors are permitted to hold, when he suddenly stopped talking and stood still.

"What's the matter, Sergeant-major?" demanded Blackie.

"Somethin' comin' our way, sir."

Blackie listened.

The sound of airplane engines which had almost died away was again audible.

"They're not coming back?"

Blackie listened with a puzzled frown.

The noise rose from throb to buzz, from buzz to angry purr.

"'Uns," said the sergeant-major' sapiently. "That's a circus—look, Sir!" He pointed eagerly. Twelve thousand feet above, the rays of the yet invisible sun caught the white wings of the enemy squadron. Tiny flecks that glittered in the dawn light and unmistakably hostile.

"Boom! Boom! Boom! Boom!"

"Pang! Pang! Pa-pa-pang!"

The sleepless Archies were at work and the skies were full of wailing.

"Oh, damn!" snapped Blackie, "every one of my machines up! Bomb-proof shelter for us, I think, Sergeant-Major."

But the sergeant-major was staring at the skies. The big German formation so perfectly alined had suddenly broken. "The leader's in trouble, sir."

No need to say as much, for the leader was sweeping earthward in wide circles.

"Ticka-tacka, ticka-tacka!"

"Machine gun—what the dickens is wrong with 'em?"

A second machine fell out of formation, disastrously blazing. The formation was now confused and scattered. Three machines had banked over and turned for home. Another three—obviously fighting machines—were circling and the fierce chatter of their guns was eloquent of their annoyance.

"But what are they fighting—one another?" demanded the mystified Blackie. "None of our people are up—glory be! There goes another!"

One of the attackers crumpled and broke in the air and spun earthward.

Then Blackie saw.

High above what had once been a formation was poised an airplane of microscopic size. It was a pin-point of light in the skies, so tiny that Blackie could not believe the evidence of his eyes until the circus turned homeward, one machine, obviously damaged and losing height with every yard it traveled, lagging in the rear.

Then did the midget in the blue condescend to give the ground observers a closer view of himself. He dived steeply on the tail of the damaged machine. They heard the splutter of his gun and saw the lame duck crash.

"But what is it—Sergeant-Major? Good Lord, it's as big as a large-sized hat-box."

The tiny stranger wheeled round, poised for a moment and then began a glide for the aerodrome.

As it drew nearer Blackie saw that his estimate of its size was not an extravagant one. It might be stowed in a big packing-case and might with no discomfort take shelter under the wing of a Handley-Page.

The midget lit lightly at the far end of the aerodrome, and Blackie ran to meet the visitor as he stepped down the few feet which separated the nascalle from the ground.

"I say, I'm awfully grateful to you, but from what toy-store did you dig out this contraption?"

The pilot shed his furry gloves and lifted the mica-eyed mask that hid his face before he spoke.

"A'll be thankin' ye, Major Blackie, sir, if ye'll no speak disrespectfully of ma wee frien', 'Annie Laurie,' the pride o' Scotland an' the terror o' the Hoon."

"Tam!" yelled Blackie, and gripped the scout by the shoulders. "Tam! You melodramatic humbug! You villain! Back again!"

"From ma honeymoon," said Tam, shaking his head, "an' just as I were gettin' used to it—mon, war's hell—have ye a seegair in your pooch—A'm travelin' wi'oot ma baggage!"

CHAPTER II

THE DUKE'S MUSEUM

When the Grand Duke of Friesruhe, son of a Most Exalted and Princely House, heir to Wilhelm XXVI of Friesruhe, beloved nephew of a Kaiser and a Czar and Colonel of the Third Regiment of the Prussian Guard, expressed his august desire to become a flying officer, permission was immediately given and instructions were issued to the Commander of the Sixty-fourth Corps District (wherein the Duke was stationed) that his Serene Highness was to be allowed to enroll himself a member of the Flying Service, might be photographed in the uniform, might indeed accompany a considerably experienced and trustworthy expert on a ground trial, providing (a) the weather were propitious, (b) the reliability of the machine had been thoroughly tested, (c) staff photographers were present, but that he must not be allowed to fly.

Whereupon the Grand Duke of Friesruhe, who was quite a nice youth, lay low, mastered the technique of the airplane with great assiduity, and on a certain day which was not propitious in the matter of weather, and in a borrowed machine which was notoriously unreliable, climbed to twelve thousand feet alone and unaided in the full view of a pallid staff, which alternately prayed and swore. In the language of court circles it was an "escapade" and the matter did not become serious until the Duke insisted upon becoming a real pilot, whereupon he was summoned to Grand Headquarters and was lectured on obedience by the Most All Highest and Then Some.

He listened to the lecture in silence, standing rigidly at attention, and went back to his principality. Within three days the socialistic Arbeiter-Zeitung published in his city began a violent agitation for Peace at Almost Any Price, and since the Grand Duke was known to be behind the Friesruhe Arbeiter-Zeitung, and the succession to the throne was secure, Grand Headquarters reversed its decision, gave him full authority to break his neck and requested that the Arbeiter-Zeitung should be subjected to Preventive Censorship.

So the Duke went joyously to the front, and the Arbeiter-Zeitung explained that what it really craved for was a Peace with Annexations and Very Large Indemnities.

That is the true story of how Colonel, the Grand Duke of Friesruhe came to be an air fighter and eventually leader of what was known on the British, French and American fronts as "The Duke's Museum."

It differed from the recognized circuses in this respect: It consisted of two flights of five machines each, and those machines were more or less freakish. All the new types of airplane that ever came to the German army were first tried out by the Museum—and in the most freakish of all it was certain that the Duke himself would be found. The Duke was the first to fly a Fokker, the first to handle a Gotha; he was the very father-in-law of the Friedrichshafen, and the comparatively successful and the comparatively useless types he handled were legion.

The cry of, "Here's the blinkin' Museum comin'!" was sufficient to empty the dugouts and bring even battalion headquarters recklessly into the open to watch twelve "machines—assorted," twelve different types of different speed and varying military values, come staggering across the sky—aerial infants learning to walk.

They were protected. High above drove the jealous scouts, buzzing like bees and relatively as large.

Many and fierce were the battles fought and many were the specimens from the Museum that crashed behind the German lines. But the Duke remained, and presently, on some fine day, our scouts would see him at the head of a straggling line of new and even more eccentric machines.

This new interest had come during the absence in England of Second Lieutenant Tam of the Scouts, and his first acquaintance with the Museum was when, returning from a reconnaissance, he barged into the ragged formation and was greeted (from the ground) by a protective barrage of "flaming onions"—the onion being a highly inflammable rocket which it is unpleasant to meet. He did not stop to investigate, having certain photographic plates which needed urgent development.

"'Twas no' a sense of duty that brought me oot a' ma coorse," reported Tam to his chief as they sat in the mess that night. "'Twas no' the quickenin' pulse of ma fichtin' ancestors—'twas the instinct that makes a wee boy push his way into the crood that surroun's a lad in a fit. Mon! but A'm keen on gettin' a squaint at the Airchduke."

"Grand Duke," corrected Blackie; "Archdukes are Austrian."

"'Tis the same, Major Blackie, sir," said Tam calmly; "Airchdukes are the grandest dukes in Austria—A'm studyin' the subject of dukes the noo. There's a bonnie book just come to me frae ma—frae a friend o' mine" (he never spoke, save in this cautious fashion, of the pretty and vivacious little American girl he had married, and who was now living in Devonshire and watching with apprehension every messenger-boy who carried a telgram); "'tis a wonderful book an' must have cost twa dollars."

"Eight shillings," corrected the youthful "ace" Bagley.

"Twa dollars, ma friend," said Tam, "an' less than eight shillin's, for the currency of ma adopted country is fine an' healthy. Well, noo, why do you interrupt me? This book is aboot war in the days before flyin' machines. They were gay times. When a commander led his flight o'er the enemy's line, he just cranked up his one-seated chairger, filled his petrol-tank wi' beer and whusky—accordin' to whether he was a squire mechanic or a knight obsairver—took a good grip of a ten-foot joystick an' said to his wee page—'Contact—let her rip, Alec;' an' off he'd zoom across the wairld, not carin' whether it snowed. An' when he met a Hun he'd ficht and ficht till he crashed him an' cut off his heid. Then by rights all the golden airmor of the Hun was his. Or, if he just brought him doon oot of control, he'd put him in a cage an' say, 'Yon feller's ma pairsonal property—his relations can buy him back for ten thousand rose-nobles.'"

"You could buy the earth and Paris if you held your prisoners to ransom, Tam," said Blackie.

"A'm no' so sure," said Tam, shaking his head; "'tis only the men-at-airms an' the young squires A've pinched, wi' an occasional baron—but barons are nothin' in Gairmany. Every Hun A've brought doon so far A've called 'Baron,' an' the only mistake A've made was when A ought to have said 'Coont' or 'Prince.' There are more barons in Gairmany than there are second loots in the British Army—they're as plentiful as Very lights on a strafe night. Suppose A held a baron to ransom, an' suppose A got through a letter to his family Slosh or Schloss, sayin'—'Dear Sair or Madame: A have found a baron bearin' your name an' address. Kindly send ransom for same in strictest confidence.' What d'ye think A'd get? A ten-cent postal stamp?"

"Get the Duke, Tam, and earn promotion," said Blackie, "he smokes the finest cigars of any man in Germany and his pockets are usually filled with them."

"He's a deid mon!" said Tam.

But a grand duke takes a lot of killing.

Tam, patrolling from Gx. 971. A. to Tm. 141 Q (you will search in vain for this hideous disguise of the limits of the Saarville district), came into contact with a flying formation which he at first identified as von Bissing's circus, usually to be found in this region. Closer inspection, however, revealed the fact that the formation was made up of "job lots" and Tam disappeared into the base of a cumulus and circled through the thick mist to pass the time which must elapse before the Museum came within fighting distance. It had been heading his way and so also had the overhead escort—five famous air-fighters formed the guard of honor.

Tam skimmed lower and lower until only the thinnest veil of mist separated him from the Grand Ducal Squadron. He judged them to be fifteen hundred feet beneath when he dived straight into the center of the formation.

Airplanes do not emit a startled squeal or roll up the whites of their eyes or shriek for help, but they have a way of illustrating emotion. They scattered and dived, some to the east, some to the north—all except, one, a new Alto-Albatross that pushed its nose up to meet the droning fury.

It was to this machine that Tam directed his attention. He passed the Albatross in a flash, something snapped behind him and a wire stay dangled loosely. He looped back to secure some of the height he had lost, but the Duke was quicker and had maneuvered for the attacking position. Tam banked over, loosing his gun and sensed the hit he made. He came again to the attack, half-circled his enemy, now enveloped in smoke, let fly another fusillade and dropped steeply for earth. Tam did not look up to discover what the German escort was doing. He knew. He dropped because he calculated that at that moment five angry machines, piloted by most redoubtable fighters were driving for him.

He fell for the cover which the flying British Archie gives to airmen in distress, but the five fell with him, for the machine of a Most Exalted Person was smoking and burning in mid-air, and each and every one of the five would be held accountable for any change in the succession to the throne of Friesruhe.

The Seventy-ninth Patrolling Flight of the United States Army witnessed these deeds from afar off and consumed with morbid curiosity came down from their lofty plane to investigate—and the chase ended.

It was the flight commander who reported, subsequently, that the Duke's machine had made a good landing.

"A'm hopin' the Duke was no' burned," said Tam, "that would be an awfu' waste o' good seegairs."

The Duke was no' burned. His incomparable Museum and Exhibiton of Mechanical Marvels and Magical Air-Conquering Apparatus paraded the Ypres front that same week with the greatest eclat, but this time (according to the report of the Umpty-ninth Squadron R.F.C. supported by the veracious "gulls" of the Royal Naval Air Service) the number of the escort was such that they darkened the sky.

The commander of the Umpty-first complained bitterly that he had lost three machines because of "this infernal obstruction" in the skies.

His machines had been good-natured bombers which were homewardly plodding their weary way, after dropping about three tons of high explosives on Roulers railway station, when they had fallen in with the Museum and its board of trustees, and three pedigreed Page machines were sorely stricken and now lay somewhere in Flanders.

Then one day, a message came through to four fighting squadrons.

"This Museum business is getting on the nerves of G.H.Q.," said Blackie to his assistant.

"What's wrong, sir?" asked that youth.

"The Museum is to be found and smudged out—its aerodrome is to be bombed at every opportunity and the Duke must be crushed."

Lieutenant Baxter whistled. "That's not like G.H.Q.," he said, "that black-hand stuff. What has the poor old Duke been doing?"

Blackie shook his head. "God knows," he said, "but it is something fierce to stir up G.H.Q.—the American and French squadrons have had the same instructions."

He opened a steel safe and took out from a drawer which he unlocked, a long yellow envelope which had been heavily sealed. From this he extracted a slip of paper on which were written about eight lines of handwriting.

"Send Tam to me," he said.

Tam was in the middle of a long composition designed for his "friend," embellished at unexpected intervals with those poems which only Tam could write. He hastily locked away his letter and hurried across to the orderly room.

"Shut the door, Tam," said Blackie—and when this was done—"what I tell you now is in absolute confidence. To-morrow we start sending out to find the Duke and he is to be brought down, if possible, within our lines. If that is not feasible, he must be crashed, and by crashed I mean his machine must be destroyed. You will tell your flight no more than this, that if necessary, you must engineer a collision in mid-air—in fact, ram him."

"Aye, sir," said Tam, gravely nodding.

"I don't know why this order has come out, but it is a very special and confidential instruction. These measures are not to be put into movement until"—he consulted the paper again—"'twelve o'clock noon on the eighteenth'—that's to-morrow."

Tam saluted and departed.

"What do you make of it, sir?" asked Baxter.

"I hardly know," replied Blackie slowly; "but from what some of the Huns we have captured say I rather fancy we have been underrating the Duke. He is one of the best, boldest and most inventive flyers in the German service. He has tried out every good machine they have had, and has made them practicable for general service. I rather fancy the big escort is more to protect him in his experiments than to save his blue blood from spilling. Remember, all his flights are carried out under war conditions."

"But what are the rest of the Museum?" asked Baxter.

"That apparently is camouflage to hide the fact that the machine that is being tried out is the one which the Duke is flying—you remember we used to do the same thing when poor Hall was alive. Hall perfected the Wingate Stabilizer at twelve thousand feet under Archie fire; he improved our bomb sights while actually circling over Treves. I rather suspect that the Duke is a genius of a similar order."

At twelve o'clock the next day, punctually to the second, the Museum came into sight to the east of St. Quentin. It consisted of ten machines flying in V-shape formation, and as usual no one machine was like another. At the apex of the V was a monoplane with an unusually long nacelle, an unusually long and remarkably narrow wing spread.

The observers, through their telescopes, reported that there was nothing more remarkable than the fact that the monoplane, in spite of its high engine power, did not lose place but maintained its position even though its companions were obviously more antiquated "buses," but most remarkable of all was the report which came through Lieutenant Gordon T. Simms, an observer of the U..S. Air Service, an extract from whose report may be quoted:

"Until engaged by enemy patrols, I had an uninterrupted view of the enemy formation, which was led by a large monoplane resembling in appearance the old Antoinette, which acted as leader. At a distance of a mile or more I saw the Antoinette machine slow until it almost stopped, the remainder of the formation passing on until ten seconds later the formation had advanced leaving the Antoinette well in the rear. It had the appearance of being almost stationary for half a minute, at the end of which time it went forward again at great speed, and took its place at the head of the formation. In the position from which I observed this, it was impossible that I could be the victim of an optical illusion."

Air experts are equally emphatic that it is impossible that an airplane can stand still without losing height. The man who invented such a machine or a pilot who could employ mechanism to produce that result would very nearly solve the last problem of aviation.

At three o'clock in the afternoon, the Museum was seen following the line of the Scarpe in a southwesterly direction, escorted by twenty battle-planes in two formations of ten. The escort was attacked by the 904th, the 623d and the 612th squadrons of the British, and by the 120th and 121st flights of the U. S. Air Services, and by de Mouleys' famous squadron of "aces"; and the battle which raged in the air has come to be historic. Fourteen German airplanes were crashed or driven down out of control and three British and one French. But in the course of the fighting the Museum got away. Again the report came through that the Antoinette had distinctly slowed her pace until she was almost at a standstill.

Following this, three British bombing squadrons raided the aerodrome where the Museum was known to reside, and dropped particularly powerful bombs upon the underground hangars—ignoring the inviting array of matchwood sheds which the Germans had erected to draw the fire of raiders.

On the twenty-first, the Museum, with the inevitable Antoinette at its head, but this time made up of much faster machines, came over the British lines and was attacked by the defensive squadrons, four of the Museum dying the death before their guardians could come to their assistance.

Again the Antoinette escaped, and bitter were the words which came humming along the wire which connected G.H.Q. with the squadrons concerned. There was a great ringing of telephone bells, and secret discussions in locked offices where eminent officers consulted in Hindustani, to the intense annoyance of the military exchange.

At eight o'clock, Blackie walked into Tam's quarters, locked the door behind him, took from his pocket a map and a large-caliber pistol of unfamiliar pattern.

Without any preliminary he began:

"The Antoinette is at the Gisors aerodrome—the experimental aerodrome to the north," he said. "We are not taking any chance with a bombing squadron. The hangar is certain to be underground. Here is a signal pistol we took from one of the Museum machines that crashed. It is loaded with a cartridge which shows a red and green light. That is the landing signal for this particular aerodrome."

Tam waited.

"G.H.Q. has heard about you and they want you to make a landing. You will probably be shot if you are caught. Here you are," he spread the map and laid his finger upon a green patch; "that is a fairly level plain about two hundred yards from the aerodrome. Land there and get into the hangar as well as you can. You will destroy the machine."

"And they will make anither," said Tam.

Blackie shook his head.

"It will take them nine months to make another like it," he said. "I have seen the Director of Intelligence. He tells me that this Antoinette is being perfected in the air, and, that the Duke is the only man that can fly it so far. You may not be able to get back to your machine," he went on, "but you must take the risk. Only use the landing light if they get an Archie barrage on you."

He shook hands and walked abruptly away. He was sending his best man to his death, and. anything he might say, now, would be feeble and inadequate. Tam looked at the map and looked at the pistol, opened his desk and took out the letter which he had just finished writing.

He added this P.S.:

"I'll be awa' to make a call on another aerodrome. Tam."

To the north of Gisors is a small aerodrome consisting of about half a dozen flimsy huts and three underground hangars which are approached by broad sloping runways. The hangars themselves are protected by nine feet of sandbagging and so elaborately camouflaged that it would be impossible to detect from the air either the runway or the bulge of earth which corresponded to the roof of the underground chambers.

In one of these were three men, two of them officers, one an old and spectacled mechanic in field-gray. The hangar was brilliantly illuminated with ground, roof and wall lights, so that there was not one bit of the long and dainty machine which stood in the center of the hangar that was not flooded with light.

The younger of the officers and, if the truth be told, the least distinguished was, contrary to all regulations, smoking a long thin cigar and eyeing the machine with knitted brows. The second of the officers, an older man and one of higher rank, was shaking his head in admiration.

"Your Highness has performed a miracle," he said; "this will rank as one of the greatest mechanical discoveries of the war."

It was the younger man's turn to shake his head. "Not yet, von Grosser," he said sharply; "you are premature. Perhaps in a month we may reduce the thing to a formula. At present I am making new discoveries every day."

He walked slowly around the machine. There was nothing extraordinary in its appearance save that, in addition to the tractor screw in front, it carried a small propeller behind the driver's seat, a propeller which was fitted at a curious angle.

"Von Missen is very anxious to make a flight in her," said the older officer. "I think he has recently arrived. I saw his landing lights a few moments ago."

"Von Missen is a fool," said his Highness, "and he would be a dead fool if he essayed it. Three times she has failed, for some reason I can not understand. But I shall get it right," he nodded; "yes, I shall get it right. If—"

"If?" repeated von Grosser.

"If the people over there," he jerked his head to the west, "don't get me."

Von Grosser laughed. "Your Highness may be assured that that will never happen," he said; "they have tried and failed. They have bombed every aerodrome between here and St. Quentin. Why," he shrugged, "I do not know."

"Because they know, my friend, that if they get me, this machine—"

He was looking at Colonel von Grosser as he spoke. The Colonel was facing the narrow entrance which admitted into the hangar when the great sliding doors were closed and he saw the other's eyebrows rise and a comical look of incredulity and annoyance dawn upon his face.

"What—"

"Hands up, all of ye!"

A figure stood in the doorway, his face half hidden by the mica goggles he still wore, puffed and padded from head to foot in a soiled yellow leather jacket.

"Come oot o' that," said Tam, "come oot, uncle!" He waved the frightened mechanic to the far wall, "which of ye is the Airchduke?" he demanded.

The younger man laughed. "I am the Grand Duke of Friesruhe," he said; "if I am the person you are seeking?"

"And is that yer fine machine?" said Tam.

"That's my fine—"

Something cracked from Tam's left hand, a blazing ball of fire leapt toward the machine, filling the hangar with a pungent and disagreeable odor. The ball struck one of the wings, which burst into a blaze.

"Thairmite," said Tam, "don't try to put it oot."

Von Grosser, paralyzed by the apparition, suddenly came to life. His hand dropped to the holster at his belt, but before he could draw his weapon Tam shot him down. The Duke had been quicker. Two bullets from his automatic went through the leather jacket of the airman before Tam's pistol could swing round and cover him.

The machine was now blazing furiously. The room was an inferno. Tam beckoned first the Duke and then the mechanic toward the little door and he himself dragged the wounded man to the safety of the little passage.

Tam led the way up the steep incline to the open air. Suddenly he turned, and with a lightning blow felled the mechanic. Then he gripped the Duke by the arm and started at a jog-trot across the aerodrome.

Dense volumes of smoke were pouring through the interstices. The alarm had already been given and the shouts of command came to them through the darkness.

"Where are you going?" said the Duke suddenly and stopped dead.

"A'm going back to ma wee bed," said Tam, "and ye're comin' wi' me."

"Then you'll take me dead," said the Duke in German and leaped at his captor.

An arm like a bar of steel flung him backward.

"By God, you shall suffer for this!" said the breathless young man.

"Oh, aye," said Tam, "d' ye no' ken me?"

"I don't want to ken you, damn you," stormed the Duke in English.

By this time they had passed through the fence wires which Tam had cut. The Scotsman was making his way with confident step toward the plain where his machine awaited him.

"A'm Tam," he said complacently; "d'ye na' ken Tam? A'm Tam, the Scoot. Noo, Duke, over yon' there's a bonnie machine wi' a nice comfortable seat for an obsairver. Will ye be my obsairver back to the British fines?"

The Duke thought a moment. "Under the circumstances, I think I will," he said.

Half-way back, and what time all the telegraph wires leading into Germany were in a condition bordering on hysteria, and while search-lights swept the skies and Archie barrages worked double time, Tam leaned over and tapped the silent figure in the observer's seat upon the shoulder.

The Duke adjusted the speaking-tube and listened.

"Hand over yeer seegairs," said Tam, remembering at this, the eleventh hour, that something was due to him.

CHAPTER III

THE KINDERGARTEN

The entry of the United States into the European war may be likened to the entry of a large and enthusiastic boys' school into a strange bathing-pond. There was a great leap, a monstrous splash, much laughter, many whoops of joy, a few yells of consternation and a considerable amount of spluttering. The experienced swimmers who were already in and were not finding the water any too fine, had been through exactly the same process before they learned the art of natation, and neither criticized nor sneered nor grew greatly hilarious, realizing that in time the hubbub would die down and there would be some desperately good swimming going on and that some of them would have to battle hard to keep abreast of the new material.

They were not all amateurs, these new arrivals. There were some who could do fine breast strokes and wonderful overhand movements and there were others who floated quite nicely. These were the "old contemptibles" of the American Army, those wise and wicked men who had sneaked away to Europe disguised as Frenchmen, Canadians, Englishmen—any old thing that gave them the right to enter the war zone.

Among the voertrekkers in the field of honor was a very considerable body of American gentlemen who were formed into a flying squadron attached to the French army and did truly wonderful work, being by nature adventurers. They earned world fame and deservedly so, for they did famous deeds which were chronicled in American newspapers and so fired the imagination of youthful America that when the big splash occurred, a large number of the swimmers made their way in the direction of those instructors in that peculiar form of warfare which is waged between the clouds and the stars.

A volume of recruits flowed into the American aerodromes to learn their business, but there was nevertheless a steady trickle of youthful talent toward France. Americans who were wintering in Egypt, Americans who were observing Paris or amusing themselves in London, very naturally directed their steps toward the American headquarters in France. They thought, and there was reason for it, that they were losing time by going to America and taking unjustifiable risks from submarines. Moreover, they were most anxious to finish the war before the other America came in, and so they filled the anterooms of the American military attachés in various cities of the world and armed with imposing passports and divers documents, they made their way to a town, which we will call Bonville, where there had been established in the twinkling of an eye the nucleus of an American Air Service.

The older men taught them the game—the stunts they found out for themselves. They did things which no reasonable and well-conducted airman should do, but everybody seemed to agree that under the circumstances those extraordinary departures from convention were wholly justified.

Tam of the Scouts was sent on a swift single-seater to make certain observations of the country which extends from the back of the British line to the sea. He was discovering landmarks whereby hostile airmen could find their way to a certain naval port. Wherever these landmarks were too conspicuous they would be camouflaged; even the course of a river, which helped a bombing squadron at night, might so be changed in appearance that it would not serve for guidance.

He reached the sea, circled over the port and headed back for his aerodrome. He was ten minutes' distance from the town, that is to say, some fifteen miles, when he was attacked in the air by a large formation which when he approached it had been orderly and regular in its appearance, but which broke and broke unpleasantly when he came within rifle-shot. Two of the machines took no part in the attack. Their pilots were firing strangely colored lights with every evidence of agitation, but the remainder came upon him like a swarm of hornets and Tam was compelled to nose-dive into the middle of them, letting off his Lewis gun and very narrowly escaping a collision with a large and old-fashioned biplane which seemed to suffer from some chronic aeronautic affliction which caused it to loop the loop involuntarily.

Tam planed down to within a thousand feet of the earth, fluttered and ruffled. It was not his business to fight people and certainly not his business to take on fifteen hostile airplanes single-handed, and as he had the foot of his enemies, he had no difficulty in shaking off all except one pursuer, who chased him back to the aerodrome and when he landed, plumped down within a dozen yards.

Tam walked across to the pilot as he was hastily unbuckling the straps about his middle and addressed him sadly: "Sirr," he said, "can ye no' tell a Hun when ye see him?"

The flushed young man who had jumped from the chaser shrieked with laughter.

"Gee," he said, "this is one on us! We thought you were a Heinie."

It transpired that Tam had butted into the kindergarten, the boldest kindergarten that had ever learned the C-A-T, cat, of aviation.

Later came Captain Bredwell of the United States Army, a teacher of the new idea and a veteran of war. He was very apologetic.

"Training a set o' pups is child's play compared with teaching these kids not to hit anything they see running loose. I tried to call 'em to heel and just as well might Noah have whistled for the dove after he had got well on his way to Ararat. I am very sorry."

"Not at all," said Blackie. "Tam enjoyed it; didn't you, Tam?"

"Weel," said Tam, "A'm no' so sure. A'll be coming over your way to morrow, sir," he said to the American officer. "What time do ye take your young gentlemen up?"

"From eleven till one, if the weather's good," said the other.

Tam nodded.

"A'll be coming about two," he said, "and ye'll recognize me by the fact that A'm wearin' a red rose in ma buttonhole and carrying the Scotsman in ma right hand."

"The kindergarten is pretty difficult to handle," confessed Captain Bredwell over the luncheon-table; "you see, we haven't had time to ground them in the fear of God and military history. They are young, they are keen, they are full of spunk but they haven't got the hang of this military business."

He shook his head reprovingly at the boy who had chased Tam back to the aerodrome, but the youth was at that moment in a heated discussion with Lieutenant Curten on the relative merits of British and American motor-cars, both, strangely enough, being the sons of men who had grown rich in exploiting the public passion for speed.

"'Tis no' discipline that young Rain-in-the-Neck wants," said Tam—he had a trick of applying the nomenclature to be found in the works of his favorite authors to those who pleased him. "'Tis a little machine-gun practise. He was on ma trail a' the time and didna get me—Mon, that's inexcusable."

"What really happened, Tam?" asked Baxter, and the babble of noise which accompanied every meal in the Umpty-fourth hushed to silence.

Tam looked over his audience as an experienced lecturer might.

"'Twas a fearfu' experience," he said. "Wingin' ma way homeward wi' no thocht o' danger, wi' a blaw sky o'erhead an' the gay green airth beneath, A was thinkin' o' you young gentlemen an' the veecious practise ye've got into of smokin' cigarettes that produce anemia, palpitation, hairt disease an' cold feet, when ma attention was attracted by the appearance on ma starboard bow of a graund aggregation of talent that would have made Buff'lo Bill tairn in his grave.

"At the moment A did not realize 'twas the United States Airmv practisin' for bluidy war. Ma first thocht was that 'twas a party of French bairdmen that had been celebratin' the feast of the Moulin Rouge."

"Say!" chuckled Captain Bredwell loyally, "that's rather tall—I guess the formation wasn't perfect, but—"

Some one whispered to him and he sat back with a grin.

"Whilst ma mind was occupied wi' givin' the merry pairty a wide miss," continued Tam, "the—what you might tairm for want of a better word—formation broke up an' the ghastly truth dawned on me."

He paused.

"'Twas a Wild West show," he said solemnly, "yes sirrs! There was buckin' broncos, an' shairpshooters, an' lasooers, an' wild Injans an' the pairformance started promptly—there was no waitin'. Whilst I was attacked on the right by Sittin' Bull an' on the left by Denver Dan, Mexican Joe dived from above, utterin' the war-cry or totem or what-not of his fierce clan. Alkali Ike tried to ram me—or tried not to ram me, A don't know which, but the result was nearly the same. The Colorado Kid caught ma controls a swat wi' his sixty-six shooter—an' A was chased to ma old log cabin by Rain-in-the-Neck howlin' for the blood of the paleface."

Tam's acquaintance with the technique of the classics was an extensive one. He went on in his singsong tone.

"Of the rest of the story there is na much to be told." he said. "Tam, the indomitable scoot, is noo an auld man wi' gray hair, an' may be seen, leadin' his grandson to the scene of his great ficht, pointin' oot the place in the sky where he was nearly straffit. Denver Dan ended his evil life in a low drinkin' shanty, Rain-in-the-Neck is a Bug Hoose, whilst the Colorado Kid got releegion an' made money."

There was terrific applause when Tam finished—loudest of all from that same Rain-in-the-Neck (in private life Cadet Cyril Yanderberg).

The story of Tam's encounter with the kindergarten became public property. From Dunkirk down to Belfort hundreds of messes recounted the story with such embellishments as fancy dictated and in a remarkably short space of time it came to the ears of Captain Fritz von Stoffel, and naturally von Stoffel was greatly interested, for he was chief of the Baby-killers' Circus.

It must be said that the babies he killed were mostly Germans. He was a disciplinarian of the fierce and fiery type. He never spoke, he barked. His lightest whisper was something between a rifle-shot and the explosion of a pop-gun. He had never raided London nor had he raided any of the villages that lie between the Kentish coast and the metropolis. Indeed he had never crossed blue water. He earned his title of Baby-killer because his specialty lay in the strafing of rest-camps, hospitals, unprotected artillery bases and observation balloons. He took few risks and in consequence endured very few casualties in air fighting; indeed, the heaviest death-roll resulted from his practise of sending nervous young pilots aloft in a high wind.

Now, most circuses are sporting. They are out looking for trouble and when they find it they get as close as they can and stay as long as it is safe, but everybody knows that von Stoffel's circus never did anything which could be exaggerated into recklessness. It so happened when the news of Tam's adventure came to the gallant captain that he had received a hint from the head-quarters of the corps to which he was attached—one of those broad Prussian hints that left a scar—that his cautiousness was developing into a vice, and it was suggested that it might be necessary to ask him to take a long leave for the benefit of his health and hand his command over to his junior.

Von Stoffel spent an evening in his stuffy and airless dugout grappling with "A Plan." That plan, set forth with much detail, was delivered into the hands of the corps commander and by him transmitted to Highest Authority, retransmitted to the corps commander with certain hieroglyphics of approval scrawled upon its margin and by him forwarded to von Stoffel, who did everything but kiss the aforesaid hieroglyphics in his ecstatic happiness.

Tam of the Scouts was ordered one fine day to take a flight into Darkest France, and pursue investigations concerning the transportation of German troops westward. Two of his machines developed engine trouble and returned and Tam went on with the two that remained and had a most exciting morning. For though his machine was a scout and not of the bombing type, he carried four bombs for exactly the same reason that the average Western citizen carries a gun in his hip pocket, and passing over a seemingly deserted aerodrome he dropped a couple to discover whether anybody was at home.

He had hardly observed the bursts before his machine was ringed with well-aimed shrapnel. Whereupon his two companions, who were quite out of the danger zone, very naturally closed into it and one of these secured a direct hit upon a building which Tam surmised must have been the private brewery of that aerodrome, for he and his companions were immediately attacked with unparalleled ferocity by the owners of the aerodrome, who had been out hunting and approached their home behind the cover which a stratum of cloud afforded.

Whereupon the three British airmen decided that it was getting very late and streaked westward, all out, losing a little height to increase the margin which lay between them and their pursuers. They passed over the line, disgracefully deserted at this particular moment by fighting craft, with six machines still in pursuit.

Now, no airman, in whatever distress of mind he may be, will fly from an enemy over his own territory, even should the enemy be overwhelmingly stronger, and in conformity with the unwritten law of air fighting, no sooner had the zigzag of trenches been left in his rear than Tam signalled "Engage" and swung round to meet his enemies.

Two modern air-planes separated at a distance of four-hundred and fifty yards approach each other at such a speed that they pass in the time that you can count six. In three of these seconds the decisive battle is fought. Either you "get" your enemy, your enemy "gets" you, or you "get" one another.

In a flash as they passed Tam saw the enemy pilot drop, and as he himself had no inclination to drop, he knew he had won, unless the enemy observer had escaped and was using the dual controls.

Imagine these two machines passing each other on a parallel course and a second later a third machine dropping from the blue and missing the tail of the attacker by inches. Picture a second British machine falling after this bolt, his gun shooting vertically earthward, along the nacelle of the diving German; imagine two other enemy machines banking over and shooting sideways and indiscriminately at Tam and his assistant—a roaring, whirling mix-up of air-planes bucking and jumping, slipping, climbing and diving, and suppose that all this happens in the space of some twenty seconds, and you visualize an air battle at its most intense period.

Tam looked down as the second machine fell in flames and began his glide to earth, for he did not need to see the remainder of the enemy flight wheel eastward to know that the battle was over. One of his own machines was going down in circles. Tam saw this and wrinkled his nose—that was the only sign of sorrow he ever showed—and there was reason enough, for that easy spiral which was bringing a dead pilot and a dead observer to earth would end in a crash.

Tam's report was almost uninteresting by the side of another report which was being flashed along the wire to Headquarters Intelligence. It was the report of a young and keen intelligence officer who had sat by the bedside of a dying German air-man, one of those whom Tam had grounded, and had listened to the unconscious man as he talked of his home in Darmstadt and his mother and the fishing on the Moselle, and how splendid it would be to go to Marienbad this summer and other things which had made the intelligence officer lean over the bed, listening intently and scribbling notes in the little book he whipped from his tunic pocket.

The air-man died before he said very much. If he had died sooner he would have saved the German army quite a number of casualties.

Tam was roused from his bed at midnight by the entrance of his superior.

"Sorry to wake you from your beauty sleep." said Blackie, putting no hint of sorrow in his voice, "but there's the greatest stunt on."

Tam sat up in bed blinking at the electric light.

"Take an interest, you sleepy devil," said Blackie.

"Oh, aye," said Tam. "A'm awfu' interested. A'm speechless wi' it."

Blackie sat himself on the bed. "The Hun is going to strafe the kindergarten to-morrow," he said; "you butted into the Baby- killers."

"You don't mean it." said Tam, wide awake. "It was no' von Stoffel?"

"It was von Stoffel," nodded Blackie, "and you interrupted a practise attack. I have always said the kindergarten flies too near the line for safety. I don't think they will after this. It is a pretty low-down thing to do, but I suppose it's fair. Von Stoffel is taking big flights to-morrow and intends swooping down on the kindergarten and there shall be a great slaughtering of innocents, according to the plan. Intelligence found it out and you are for the stunt," he shook his head mournfully. "You are a lucky beggar," he said; "I don't mind admitting that I asked to go in your place, but my life is much too valuable."

"What is the stunt?" asked Tam.

Blackie chuckled. "The kindergarten will remain in school to- morrow," he said, "their places in the air will be taken by the aces. All the squadrons in this part of the world are to send one. You are the representative of the Umpty-fourth."

Tam swung his legs out of bed.

"There's no need to get up," said Blackie, "the stunt isn't on for another nine hours."

"Mon," said Tam. unbuttoning his pajama jacket, "'twill take me that time to learn the American language."

At five o'clock in the morning two specially chosen patrols flew to the region of the kindergarten's aerodrome and began sweeping the skies eastward, forming a barrage through which no inquisitive Hun might pass. They were not protecting the kindergarten, far from it. They had a certain duty to perform and when that was performed, as it was by eight o'clock, the patrols signalled one another good-by and departed for their homes, leaving the way clear for von Stoffel, who was due at eleven, that being the hour when the kindergarten took the air.

But between five and eight the aces began to arrive, sweeping down from great heights and ranging themselves in nice orderly lines on the broad expanse of the aerodrome. Tam was the first to arrive. De Rochleaux, with twenty-nine crashed to his credit, was the second. Mildred of the Hundred and Umpty-first Squadron, who had on one memorable occasion taken on a circus single-handed and had brought down six machines, was the third, and after his arrival the aces fell thick and fast.

Le Fevre, Runnymede, Lord Arthur Saxman, Townly, the American instructor with eighteen skull-and-cross-bones painted on the nose of his machine to represent the eighteen sad occurrences to the German Army, Minter "the guardian of Ypres"—they all met for breakfast, full of joy at the forthcoming meeting. They took the air at 10:15, flying raggedly, the most beautiful piece of camouflage that was ever seen in the air.

At exactly the same hour von Stoffel snapped the case of his great gold watch and remarked to his obsequious adjutant: "Before we come back the American correspondents will have something to write home about."

He glanced down at the long line of airplanes, pilots in their places, mechanics standing by the propellers, and raised his hand in a signal. Instantly there was a roaring and snorting, thudding and thundering din of engines. His hand dropped and his graceful Fokker leaped forward and zoomed up at an acute angle. One after the other the squadron followed and ten minutes later the formation was in being.

Von Stoffel, sitting in the cock-pit before the pilot, fired his signal pistol and the big circus moved westward. The German commander adjusted his ear-piece and speaking-tube, fired off a few rounds from his gun to test it and then gave himself up to the enjoyable prospect before him.

The circus crossed the British lines and were greeted by Archie in the usual manner. Von Stoffel, his powerful field-glasses to his eyes, searched the distant heavens.

"Ah! There they are," he said triumphantly, and signaled "Enemy in Sight."

"We shall have to climb," said a voice in his ears, the voice of his squadron's crack pilot, "they are much higher than we."

"What are we flying at?"

"Ten thousand feet, Herr Captain; they are at twelve thousand."

This was hitch number one. The reconnaissance patrols which von Stoffel had sent out had reported that the kindergarten never flew higher than eight thousand feet. The baby-killer signaled a change of direction and asked for altitude and the big formation began climbing. Again the direction was changed.

"They are climbing too," said the voice of his pilot. "I think they are going up to fifteen thousand."

Von Stoffel swore and again his squadron climbed.

The spurious kindergarten watched these maneuvers with the greatest hilarity. Lord Arthur Saxman, by reason of his seniority, commanded the right wing.

"Bags I the great white chief," he said joyously and went down in an alarming nose-dive, working both his guns—for he was a two-gun man and ambidextrous.

"That big bomb for mine!" said Captain Bredwell and dropped simultaneously.

"Big fellow, I want ye," and Tam dropped, his gun rapping furiously.

This was all very hard luck on von Stoffel, because either of these aces could have settled him.

Of the twenty-two strafers that set forth to beat up the kindergarten, four came back, two limping, if a knocking engine be the equivalent to a limp, and a German communiqué of that night read:

"WE CONDUCTED A SUCCESSFUL RAID UPON AN AMERICAN AVIATION CENTER. SEVERAL MACHINES WERE SEEN TO FALL IN FLAMES. ALL OUR MACHINES RETURNED SAFELY."

This telegram, thoughtfully transmitted from headquarters to the kindergarten mess, where they were entertaining the noisiest bunch of guests that had ever assembled, embellished the end of a perfect day.

CHAPTER IV

BILLY BEST

Tam of the Scouts sat enthroned on the edge of the billiard table—which, appropriately enough, since he formed the topic of conversation, was a luxury donated by the Splendiferous Lieutenant Walker-Mannsell whose paternal relative was reputed to have so much money that he had refused war contracts. This Splendiferous One, still spoken of by the squadron with affection and amusement, lay in a little grave to the west of Mossy Face Wood, and that the squadron joked about him is accounted for by the fact that the men of the R.F.C. never die, and, accordingly, are never invested with solemn post-mortem virtues designed to prove that they were really too good to live.

Therefore he was "The Splendiferous One" and "S.W.M." and men roared over the jokes told against him—and if they always ended the story with "good old Splendif, he was a lad of the village"—why, they would have done the same if he had been just outside the mess-room.

"A call to mind an argument wi' Mr. Walker-Mannseel," said Tam. (Observe that Tam was a sergeant when the boy was living and Tam regarded it as extremely disrespectful to quote the nickname he would never have employed to one who was his superior.) "'Twas hoo much an ordinary spendthreeft could spend in a day if he'd gie his mind to it—A said five dollars, but the wee lad rather thocht that if a body corn-centrated he micht spend seex."

"Good old Splendiferous," said Blackie, laughing with the rest; "but you haven't told us what happened to Goldheimer."

Tam had begun the story of the magnificent Goldheimer and had drifted through a dissertation on plutocracy in the field, to one of the best loved of his officers.

"Goldheimer" had been born Thysen-Hyndorpf. He had been born with a steel ingot in his mouth, for his parent had been the veritable Theodore Thysen, the Westphalian steel baron. His brother officers had named him Goldheimer and even worse, and in due course the fame of him came to the right side of the line, and his photograph, cut from a Berlin society journal, adorned the green notice-board of the mess of the Umpty-fourth.

There he smirked, with his stout, vacant face, his stiff little mustache, his tiny monocle, his imposing Pickelhaube, and men of the patrol on their way to the sheds would stop and examine the features thoughtfully and wonder if it was their luck to get him that day.

Goldheimer was rich—rich beyond the dreams of actresses. He was so rich that if he had written down his fortune in marks he would have had writer's cramp before he reached the last cipher.

He was so offensively rich that every hard-up subaltern of the R.F.C. pined for his destruction.

" 'Twas no' like the lad to be oot before the air was war-m," said Tam, resuming his narrative at the point where it had been diverted, "an' ye may imagine ma surprise, when passin' to the sooth o' Cambrai—at the place where the Hoon has five or six bridges across the canal—to obsairve the expensive ootfit of Mc Goldheimer riskin' the mornin' air. There was no mistakin' him. His seelver-mounted wings, the graund gold monogram on his silken wings, the filigree fusilage by Mr. Benny Vinturo, the heavy di'mond buckles to his stays, the jeweled engine an' the gun-metal gunwork of his gun. 'Tam,' says A to mesel', 'are ye no' ashamed to be seen oot in the same sky as yon? Awa' wi' ye!' A says, 'be off an' brush yeer pants an' change yeer cravat—look at Mc Goldheimer,' A says, 'take a lesson from him—follow him,' A says—so A followed.

"He sat in his seat a fine figure of a man. His surtout or haubeck was of some clingin' material that clung. Aboot his shapely heid was a broad band of dull gold richly encrusted wi' uncut rubies; a simple collar of celluloid an' mother-of-pairl or father-of-concrete completed the picture.

"A dived for to make his acquaintance. But he was prood. The haughty intolerance which comes from generations spent in the board-room cuttin' down expenses would not allow him to unbend. He side-flopped wi' dignity, but A was no' to be shaken off.

"'Ma mannie,' says' A, 'do ye no' ken that Tam o' the Scoots is on yeer trail? Have ye no creepin' sensation up an' down yeer spine to tell ye that the terror of the cloods is stayin' wi' ye?' Apparently not. Wi' the courage of despair the reckless millionaireman tairned on his remorseless pursuer, his coorse face inflamed wi' drink, high livin' an' annoyance. He glared at his persecutor, the gold fillin's of his teeth quiverin' with passion.

"Glancin' scornfully at his puny opponent he banked o'er and got the sun* of his absent-minded but resourceful foe. 'Twas a contest that Homer or Rudyard Kiplin' would have taken the elevator to see. Capital an' labor battled in the cloods. The hated money classes an' the sweatin' proletariat joined issues. The idle rich—an' no' so idle wasn't that lad as ye'll notice, if ye take a squint at the wings of ma wee Kitten—the idle rich an' the haggard toiler, alone, or nearly alone, under the watchin' stars, focht that the wairld should be made safe for democracy.

[* "Getting the sun" is to get between the sun and your enemy.]

"It ended a' too soon," said Tam sadly. "A came down in a fine dive an' loosed ma last drum at the diamond sun-burst he wore on the back of his neck an' he responded. Instantly gold bullets was hailin' aboot my ears. If A'd stayed long enough A'd have died a millionaire. Dazzled an' blinded A broke off the unequal contest an' dropped slowly to airth."

"Which means that Goldheimer's patrol got on your tail and strafed you?" suggested Baxter.

"Aye—something like that," admitted Tam; "there were ten o' the lads—Tam could have tackled nine— but the fearless boy fra' Glasgow was outnumbered."

"Goldheimer putting on frills?" somebody asked and Tam smiled.

"A'd be sorry to lose the wee feller—he's a graund practise for the young an' inexperienced aviator."

In real life, whatever may be the case in fiction, the multi-millionaire, even though he may have inherited his fortune, is very infrequently a fool. He may generally be distinguished by his uneasiness, his suspicion and that shrewd business ability which we associate with confidence men. Nor are stout young men who affect monocles and wear ridiculous mustaches necessarily brainless, lethargic and addicted to the four a.m. habit.

Goldheimer was a notable illustration of the fact that great possessions sometimes go hand in hand with great mental capacities.

Many crack pilots, French and British, had gone out to say how d'ye do to the Goldheimer patrol and had come back more cracked than ever. He was fat but nippy. His eye was glassy, but behind the sights of a machine-gun it had all the robust qualities of the big game hunter. He was ridiculous but his airmanship was sublime. The scalps of seventeen British machines hung to his bomb-proof wigwam and he was always out to add to his collection.

"As like as not the puir lad'll be shot down by an Archie that's aimin' at somethin' else," said Tam, "or he'll fall to the kindergarten—"

"Which reminds me," said Blackie, looking up from his cards, "I am going to plant a Hun** on you."

[*"Hun" is a term applied to all aviation recruits.]

"A Hun!" said Tam is consternation.

Blackie's eyes twinkled as he nodded.

"Cadet William Best of the United States Army," he said. "They are breaking up the kindergarten and attaching one youngster to each of the French and British squadrons. As a matter of fact," he went on, "you will find William quite a pleasant young man, he has already had some air-fighting experience. He attached himself to the Camelot Squadron about six months ago and though he has not undergone his full technical course, he is a pretty wise bird."

Tam had got down from the billiard table and was looking dolefully at his superior.

"Am A to understand, Major Blackie, sir, that A must teach this young gentleman controls?"

"No, no, Tam," laughed Blackie, "not so bad as that. You will just give him tips on air fighting. From what I have heard of him he does not require much tuition. Be at the office to-morrow morning at ten o'clock and I will introduce you."

At that hour Tam met his pupil. He was young, very young. His face was fresh and pink like a girl's, his gray eyes, full of laughter, were lit with those eager fires which God kindles in children to warm the ashes of their parents' hearts.

"This is Cadet Best," introduced Blackie; "this is Second Lieutenant McTavish who will take you under his wing."

"Glad to meet you," said Cadet William Best joyously and extended a large, firm hand.

Tam and his charge surveyed one another in an amused silence.

"That is all," said Blackie after an embarrassing pause.

Tam jerked his head to his companion and they passed out of the office.

"Have ye a bed, sir?" asked Tam.

"Sure—I carry one around in my grip," said the cheerful youth.

"What A mean," said Tam, "have ye a place to lay yeer weary heid if ye survive the dangers an' perils o' the elements?"

Cadet William Best grinned and shook a head which in its bright-eyed alertness showed no signs of weariness.

"Weel," said Tam, "ye'll bunk wi' me. If ye leave the door open an' sleep wi' yeer feet oot o' the window there'll be room for ye."

No other word was spoken. Tam led the way with dignity, opened the door of his quarters and ushered his friend into the little room.

"Do ye smoke?"

"Sure."

"Would ye like a seegair?"

"Try me."

Tam thought a while. "Yeer too young for seegairs," he said; "they try the nairves an' weaken the nairvous system—A'll give ye a stick o' candy."

He groped under his bed and produced a large box of familiar tint and embellishment. This he opened, disclosing a platoon of large cigars lying stiffly at "attention" wearing the gold and scarlet waist-belts of their caste.

"Perhaps ye'd better smoke," said Tam gloomily; "they cost one franc twenty-five per, an' A doot if they're paid for."

"Fine," said Mr. Best enthusiastically; "these look good to me—where do you buy 'em?"

"A dinna buy seegairs," said Tam. "They're donated by ma friends, admirers—an' pupils."

"I get you," nodded the other, puffing luxuriously.

"A'm a prood an' tetchy feller," said Tam; "ye must no' hairt ma feelin's by handin' 'em to me in a coorse an' brutal manner. Ye must just leave 'em aroond careless an' A'll find 'em—yeer name is William, A doot?"

"William," agreed the pupil.

"A'll be callin' ye Billy," said Tam; "'tis a nickname A've invented. Ye'll be Billy Best—no, ye'll be Boy Billy Best inside this room so that ye may retain a sense of ma superiority in age, morals an' proved efficiency. Ye may call me Tam an' ye may sleep on that bed when the sheets are changed."

"Where will you sleep?" demanded Billy Best with a hint of truculence in his tone.

Tam rubbed his chin. "A'll sleep on the floor—A prefair it. A've never slept in a bed in ma life. Gie me a heap o' slag an' a couple o' bricks an' A wouldna' call the king ma uncle."

Billy drew at his cigar deliberately.

"You may can all that sleeping-on-the-cold-ground stuff," he said; "the floor for mine—I'm a hog-sleeper. Nothing short of a head-on collision wakes me and I prefer broken glass to Ostermoors."*

[An American matress brandname.]*

"A could never sleep in a bed," protested Tam; "'tis effiminate practise an' weakens the army's morale."

The timely arrival of the quartermaster sergeant with a fatigue party and a second bed put an end to the discussion.

It was after this was installed and the heavy-footed mechanics had departed that Billy Best, acquainting himself with his new surroundings, discovered things behind a cretonne curtain—four rows of shelf tightly packed with literature; not the commonplace literature stiffly bound and consistently neglected which you would find in a library of the literary dilettante; not the musty tomes that decorate the study of the professor, but bright, vital, red-blooded stories between paper covers of lurid design.

Tam was writing at his table when he heard a gasp and looking up, went very red, for Billy Best, his eyes blazing with joy, was examining a twenty- four page monograph devoted to the life and death of Yellowstone Jim who was (as the explanatory subtitle revealed) The Lone Bandit of Crow's Nest Canyon.

"Ye'll no' want to be readin' that stuff," said Tam uncomfortably—he was a little sensitive with strangers; "they belong to a young frind o' mine."

"Do you mean to say you haven't read them?" asked the amazed youth. "See here—if you haven't, make a start. This is the only stuff worth reading. You can have your Scotts and Dickenses and Thackerays—this is meat."

"Weel," said Tam, "A'll no' say A haven't glanced through these degradin' wairks of fiction."

"Aw!" grunted the boy, "degrading nothing—this is life! Look at this one, 'The Pawnee Cache or Black Dick's Fight for Fortune'—one of the best yarns—"

"Mon, it's easy to see ye've no' read—here gie me the books—here it is. 'Mollie the Moorman or The Thugs of Utah'—when ye're talkin' aboot stories will ye cast yeer eye o'er that yin!"

Tam was excited now—Billy Best's voice was raised to a key of dispute.

"You're nutty, Tam! This Pawnee Cache yarn—"

We may leave them to their disputation. Wiser men, men grown gray in the service of Arts and Letters, have argued as fiercely and with less kindliness over matters in no sense more important.

At ten o'clock the next morning Tam and his new assistant took the air—Tam at the controls, Billy in the cockpit for'ard.

Tam's plan was to spend the morning in stunts. He outlined the program after breakfast.

"We'll acquaint ye with the spinnin' nose-dive, the windmill loop, the tail dive, the oot o' control dive, the stall an' the fa' an' ither pretty exercises."

"Bully," said Billy.

"It's verra dangerous," cautioned Tam.

"I'll bet you won't hurt Tam," said Billy, "and if you don't hurt Tam you won't hurt Billy."

"Sometimes," said Tam, "the controls go wrang—sometimes when one's thinkin' o' trouble doon drops the Imperial Gairman Circus "

"Circuses arc my vice," said Billy, speaking with some difficulty.

"A'm no' so sure o' yeer judgment," said Tam before the start; "but A like yeer appetite—do ye ever stop eatin,' Billy?"

Billy blushed guiltily and almost choked in swallowing the chunk of candy that was bulging his cheek.

"My people send me lots of candy," he said apologetically; "it helps pass time between smokes."

"It takes attention from the wairk," said Tam sternly; "ha' ye any in yeer pooch?"

Billy meekly produced from the pocket of his leather jacket a sticky mass so completely at one with its paper wrapping that it was difficult to tell where paper ended and candy began.

Tam took it with a grimace of disgust, bit it in two and handed the other half to its owner.

"Do you like it?" asked Billy anxiously.

"A have no' finished eatin' through the paper," mumbled Tam; "in wi' ye!"

He pushed the machine steeply upward, grinned as he saw the boy handling the gun in the bow and cast his hopeful eyes round to left and right for something to kill, and banked to reach a cloud base.

His scheme was to go through the mist "all out"—an unnerving experience for the tyro—and to end with a nose fall. He opened up, hit the cloud and was instantly engulfed in a blind white mist, so dense that glancing back he could only catch occasional glimpses of his tail.

The gloom, at first hardly noticeable, increased in density. From pale gray the light went yellow, umber and then a blackness as of night.

Tam glanced at his compass and brought the head of his machine to the north; but three minutes passed without the darkness lessening. It was not an unusual experience for Tam, whatever it might be for the boy in the cockpit. The density and width of clouds are difficult to gage, particularly when they are approached at their own level.

Another minute passed and Tam moved the joy-stick. The nose of the machine dropped and down, down roared the big airplane.

Billy had a momentary sensation of sickness, but that passed. He felt that nature with her trick of improvising conditions to meet circumstances had rearranged his digestive system so that it should be as near as possible to his throat. He moved his head slightly to get a better view of the nothingness which was leaping to meet him, and the pressure of the air nearly wrenched his head from his neck. Then the blackness blended swiftly with umber-yellow-gray, and Billy was looking down at a neat little world all checkered with fields and laced with white roads. Also, there were five airplanes about a thousand feet beneath and each of these bore on its wings that strange device, a black iron cross.

If the truth be told there was nothing auriferous or magnificent in the appearance of Goldheimer's patrol. There were neither silver fittings nor gold mountings nor jeweled holdings. It was just a business-like collection of fighting planes. Tam knew it—Billy knew nothing except that This Was the Life.

"Gun!" wheezed a voice through the speaking tube; "aim between ... pilot ... obsairver ... tak' the left-hand machine ... don't tak' yeer eyes off him till he crashes."

Billy Best adjusted his sights with a jerk of his hand.

"Fire!" thundered a voice in his ear and Billy fired.

The leader's machine put up her tail and dropped, Tam in pursuit, four enemy machines behind him.

"He's smokin', Billy!" yelled the voice in the speaking tube; "hit him anither crack an' get ready to shoot up."

Billy was obeying when the machine turned over and slipped sideways. He looked round and met the goggled eyes of Tam—or one eye, for the other was screwed up in a ferocious wink. Another machine was swooping and Billy brought up the muzzle of his gun and sent a shower of nickel ripping through the canvas of the wing. Amateurs' luck is proverbial. Before he knew what had happened or realized that he had brought it about in some mysterious way, the wing of the attacker collapsed. It leaped up as though it had been struck by a gigantic hammer from beneath.

Round went Tam's machine to avoid the debris—there was a momentary glimpse of a falling body, of two figures helmeted and masked, of a big white tail ornamented with iron crosses—and then nothing.

Tam had maneuvered for height, but the three enemy machines had reformed and were full of fight.

The little pilot weighed the chances and decided in favor of an early lunch. He feinted to climb, then, without warning, dropped earthward, skimming over the lines and rising only sufficiently to clear the avenue of poplars two miles beyond which the aerodrome lay.

He unstrapped himself and assisted Billy Best to land.

"Weel?" he asked.

Billy's face was sad, his tone querulous. "Why didn't you let me finish the others?" he demanded.

Tam looked him over before replying. "D'ye ken what ye've done this morn, ma lad?" he asked.

"Sure—I've brought down two machines, but—"

"Does it penetrate to that desolation ye call a mind, that ye've strafed the greatest Gairman airman, bar Richtofen?"

The eyes of Billy Best lit up. "Richtofen—he's the Big Thing, isn't he?" he asked eagerly.

"The biggest," said Tam.

"Where's he to be found?" demanded the boy.

Tam removed his leather helmet and wiped his brow. "Do ye want to go up noo—an' look for him?"

"Sure thing—why not?"

"Haund over that stick o' candy ye're hidin'—an' behave," said Tam sternly.

And they went over to the office together to report, chewing industriously.

CHAPTER V

THE WAGER OF RITTMEISTER VAN HAARDEN

There is among the children of all countries, and this has been true through all the ages, a certain test of courage which varies according to locality and according to the standard which local tradition demands. Blessed indeed is the boy of that town which has a suicide's tree to which shivering youth can make a midnight pilgrimage, bringing back proof of his valor; or great deeds can be accomplished and prowess proved beyond any question, if there are inaccessible cliffs which may be climbed, what time parents are blissfully unconscious of the narrow margin which separates the smoothness of their daily life from the upheaval consequent upon a fashionable funeral.

Not so many years ago the small boys of the village demonstrated at once their agility and daring by making lightning dashes across the path of motor-cars, he who missed the mud-guard by the narrowest space being acclaimed a hero, and holding his position until some rival who strove to emulate his deed, miscalculated the distance and made that form of test unpopular amongst the mothers of the village.

Cadet William Best was standing beside his Hepworth Kitten gazing a little dubiously at the sky when Tam crossed the aerodrome in his direction.

"Ye're goin' up. Billy," said Tam solemnly. "A thocht A'd come and say good-by to ye."

Billy Best, who was chewing gum with extraordinary regularity, made no reply. His eyes were wistfully fixed upon a streak of cloud which was passing all too quickly across the heavens

"Ye're a good boy as far as ye go," Tam went on in his most sepulchural tones. "There's a grand poem that A've got in ma heid for ye.

"Puir Billy Best
Is noo at rest,
He's burnt somewhere handy.
We'll miss his face
Aroond the place,
But oh! we'll miss his candy!"

"Say," said Billy between bites, "were you ever cheerful?"

"'Tis a lang way ye're goin'." said Tam, ignoring the question, "on a bit machine that has no parteecular merit except that ye canna be seen if ye get behint a machine-gun bullet. The air-r is filled'wi' skeelful and cunning Huns—A doot if A'll ever see ye again. Did ye leave the seegairs where I could find 'em?"

Billy jerked his head to the waiting mechanic and stepped gingerly into the fuselage.

"Before ye go," said Tam, "do ye know yer way?"

"Aw! Rats!" snarled Billy Best. "Contact!"

The mechanics swung the propeller round once, twice, and then it caught hold with a surprisingly loud roar for so small an engine.

Tam stood with a smile in his eye as the little Kitten zoomed steeply up from the aerodrome. He watched it circling for height, and then, a tiny speck in the sky, he saw it turn and make toward Mossy Face Wood. He was in his own machine in two seconds and was climbing as steeply after his friend before the speck which represented the Kitten was out of sight.

Tam's scout was the fastest of the squadron. He might reasonably hope to overtake Billy before Mossy Face Wood was reached, but he made no such attempt, keeping well to the left and crossing the line just below Quéant.

It was not until a quarter of an hour later that he saw Billy. Even then he would not have spotted him but for the fact that the air above Mossy Face Wood was filled with white and black shell-bursts.

Tam circled round and came to the east of the wood, and, looking down, saw the swift Albatross squadron climbing up to engage the intrepid disturber of their peace, for Billy had evidently carried out his promise, had dived to the sacred aerodrome and had loosed his machine gun at the indignant members of the chasing squadron lined up ready to rise.

Tam dipped for the nearest machine and sent it down out of control. Billy was now on the home stretch and there was nothing to be gained by waiting for certain trouble, for some of the Mossy Face squadron were certain to be in the upper regions of the air and moving in a fury to cut off the raiders.

Billy reached home a few seconds ahead of his companion and came down with one smashed strut, divers injuries to his wings, a leaking radiator and a groggy elevator. Otherwise he was sublimely happy, for he had climbed the cliff and visited the haunted tree and crossed ahead of the motor-car. In other words, he had bearded the Mossy Face squadron in its lair, a feat which all good young airmen accomplish if they have the opportunity.

His face was radiant and shining with pardonable pride when Tam came over to him.

"Bad luck, Billy," said Tam; "you didn't get there, I see!"

Billy stared at him.

"Didn't get there?" he demanded wrathfully. "What do you mean? Of course I got there. I dived to within five hundred yards of the ground...a dozen machines came up after me...I loosed my gun—"

"Did ye noo?" said Tam incredulously. "Noo watching the ficht close at hand I thocht ye were intercepted by the watchful Hun. 'Puir Billy,' ses A, 'brave lad,' ses A to mesel."

"Did you see me?" demanded Billy heatedly.

"Oh, I saw ye," admitted Tam.

"Did I go down over Mossy Face Wood?"

"Ye did," said Tam.

"Very well then," said the triumphant Billy.

"Ye did," repeated Tam, "and ye owe me the box of seegairs A bet ye."

An outrageous claim which left Billy speechless.

Now the relationship between the Imperial Flying Corps of the German army and the flying corps of their enemies is a remarkable one. There are no written laws, no verbal arrangements, no discussions and agreements which bind other parties to any of the curious laws which have grown up in the course of the war and which govern both sides equally. For example, it had never been arranged that the flight over the aerodromes east of Mossy Face Wood should be regarded as a test of the quality and courage of British or American airmen, and no reciprocal arrangement had been reached by which the aerodrome of the Umpty-fourth should serve the same purpose for the recruits of Boelke's or Immelman's squadrons. It was "understood;" but how that understanding was reached is a mystery, that the post-graduate course of flying should include the difficult exercise represented by a trial flight from one aerodrome to the other.

It was understood too, that by way of signaling his arrival at the enemy goal, the student should endeavor to the best of his ability to shoot or bomb any odd gentleman of the squadron who happened to be in billets or in the open below, and it was equally understood that if the aerodrome thus attacked succeeded in shooting or driving down the rash visitor so that he crashed to his death, the side which obtained this success scored one.

The rivalry between Mossy Face Wood and the Umpty-fourth was a particularly keen one at the moment when Billy Best went out and returned in safety. For the scores stood:

Umpty-fourth, 26
Mossy Face, 12

and two of the latter were accounted for by defective engines and were not seriously included by the enemy in his calculation.

Indeed, the German airman is, speaking largely, a good sportsman. All that is best in the German army has gravitated to the flying corps, which in the third year of the war was the corps d'élite.

So much so that it ranked in social prestige above the Grenadiers of the Guard who hold a terribly high position in the military hierarchy.

Major Blackie duly recorded in his unofficial diary the fact that Billy had come and gone, and anticipating the sequel to this successful visit at a moment when the Mossy Face crowd were naturally feeling sore, he sent up a flight to patrol the area between Mossy Face and the Umpty-Fourth, and the precaution was justified, for at five o'clock that evening two German candidates for honor came speeding through the air at twelve thousand feet en route for the Umpty-fourth, followed at a distance by interested veterans who came to see the fun.

The first of the candidates was shot down two thousand yards west of the Umpty-fourth headquarters. The second reached the aerodrome and dropped a gas bomb, fell into a nose dive to avoid the attention of an aerial sentinel above and was shot down at six thousand feet by Tam who was climbing up to meet him.

So that at the end of that day the score was:

Umpty-fourth, 28
Mossy Face, 12

It was just about this date that Rittmeister von Haarden made his appearance upon the scene. In the chilly hours before the dawn, when the sky was smothered with stars and the world was still save for the never-ending thud and thunder of the guns, Tam led his flight over the lines for a three-hour reconnaissance. Four machines took part in the enterprise, and the pilots beside himself were Billy Best, Feltham and Barnstable.

They crossed the line in the dark and were some hundred miles from their base when the first rays of the sun glittered upon the white wings of the four planes. They were over a world which was singularly free from the evidence of war, a world of green checkered fields, of meandering threads of rivers, of clustering hamlets, though far away to the northwest a dull smudge of gray smoke and mist advertised the existence of a large industrial town.

There were no enemy machines in sight but the main roads were filled with transports, and Tam detected and photographed a big naval gun, admirably camouflaged, before a battery of Archies opened on his party and sent the machines rocking southward.

The light was not good for photography and much of the work was simple note-taking. They were searching for a cavalry concentration which was supposed to have come into existence in this particular area, and presently they found it, mile upon mile of white tents and picket-lines.

Since his duty was not to attack but to observe, Tam's survey was a cautious one. By this time the light had improved and the cameras were clicking busily.

At seven o'clock Tam fired the "Return" signal, and the four scouts turned homeward, devoting the next ten minutes to a very careful test of their guns—for between them and their aerodrome lay some thirty squadrons of expert aerial fighters.

The morning, however, was clouding up and reconnoitering airplanes climbed until they were within reach of cover if cover were necessary. The necessity soon became apparent. Little white dots showing against the gray-blue of the horizon began to make their appearance.

It was within the cover afforded by clouds that Tam made his first acquaintance with Rittmeister von Haarden. He was going full lick through an impenetrable wall of white fog when something leaped out of the cloud before him and passed in a flash. He had a momentary glimpse of a great Albatross, the wings of which missed his by a few yards and that was all.

The tremendous disturbance of air caused by the machine's passing made him side-slip out of the cloud into the visible range of the anti-aircraft guns. He looked round and saw a machine, which he recognized as Billy Best's, rocking and diving amidst a veritable tornado of shell. Even as he looked the firing ceased and Tam banked over, for he knew that somebody was being attacked in the air and it was within the range of possibility that that somebody was himself. He glanced side-wise and saw the big Albatross dropping straight for Billy, glimpsed the stabbing pencils of flame from its machine gun and came round on a hairpin turn to engage the enemy. He and Billy were alone. The other two machines were in the cloud, quite unconscious of the fact that he was being attacked.

But the Albatross had apparently no friends in the offing. Billy stalled and looped behind his assailant as Tam got one burst of fire at the enemy. But the man in the Albatross was no amateur. His red-and-green striped wings dipped in a nose dive, a red ball of fire leaped from the fuselage, and Archie opened almost instantly upon the two British machines.

"This," said Tam, "is where we gang hame," and "gang hame" he did, avoiding all further combats, dodging the furious barrage which was put up against him behind the lines and reaching the aerodrome in time for breakfast.

"Captain Blackie. sir," he reported (he consistently ignored the major's promotion), "there's a new feller wi' a gay Albatross painted like a sun-blind."

"Von Haarden," said Blackie; "I heard he is on this sector. You had better watch that fellow. He is the best man the Germans had on the Russian front."

"Puir lad," said Tam shaking his head; "it's an awfu' come down from Russia to Somewhere-Near-Amiens. A doot he'll miss the wee Bolchyvicks. 'Twill be a sad change after the glorious uncairtainties of war on the eastern front, not knowing whether ye'll be treated better if ye fall on one side of the line than if ye fall on the other."

"Make no mistake, Tam," warned Blackie, "this fellow is an ace. We shall see him over here—Boelke makes all his new men do that stunt."

"A'll be verra glad to meet him, and so will ma wee frien' Billy Best," said Tam loyally.

"How is that boy shaping?" asked Blackie.

"He's a fine lad," said Tam soberly. "You may think I'm prejudiced because he's a fellow Scotsman."

"Eh?" asked the startled Blackie.

"A fellow Scotsman," said Tam calmly. "D'ye think he's American because he was born of American parents in America? There ye're wrong, Captain Blackie. Speeritually he's Scots."

Blackie smiled. "You're not going to entangle me into the realms of metaphysics, Tam," he said; "I warn you and your Scots friend to look out for this fellow."

"Warn him," said Tam; "he'll need it. A'm going to tell Billy about him."

Tam shared a "bunk" with Cadet William Best, and here he found that young man stretched at full length on his bed, a suspicious-looking bulge in his mouth, his eyes glued to a paper-covered volume.

"Get up, ye lazy deevil," said Tam sternly. "Mon. if ye'd heard the things that Captain Blackie was saying about ye'."

"About me?" mumbled Billy.

"Don't speak wi' yer mouth full," said Tam. "Have ye no got over that disgustin' habit of yours? Billy, it's childish for a grown man to be chewin' goodies like a wee bairn. Faugh! Let's open the window. The place reeks wi' the faint sickly fumes of mint. Have ye eaten it all?"

Billy meekly produced a solid slab of unhealthy-looking sweetmeat and Tam nipped off a generous quantity before he spoke with the same difficulty which Billy was experiencing.

"'Tis no' so good as the last lot," he complained; "yeer parents are neglectin' ye."

"What did Blackie say about me?" demanded the youth on the bed.

"A'd like to spare ye," said Tam, seating himself at his desk and extracting a report form. "A did ma best for ye, Billy, but though A'm puir A'm honest."

"Pure?" asked the puzzled Billy.

"Impecunious," said Tam. "'What likes yon American boy?' ses Captain Blackie. 'He's verra young but he'll lairn,' ses I. 'Are ye lookin' after him?' ses Blackie. 'A am. sair,' ses I. 'Every morning A make him wash his neck and clean his teeth, and look after him as if he was ma own child.' 'He's a rotten flyer, A'm thinkin,' ses Captain Blackie."

"He didn't say that?" said Billy in alarm.

"Not exactly in those words," said Tam, "but from the look in his eye, A kent that was what he meant. 'He's no' so bad,' ses I; 'Give him another chance,' ses I; 'his nairves aren't all they might be,' ses I. 'But that's due,' ses I, 'to his practise of smoking seegairs.' 'Do something for him, Tam,' ses he; 'persuade him to give them up, Tam,' ses he. 'take 'em away from him, if necessary by force,' ses he, 'and keep 'em till he comes of age.' 'A will,' ses I."

"You won't," says Billy Best resuming his study of exciting literature. "I've already given up smoking twice at your request. I thought it was bully of you to take such an interest till I found you smoking 'em."

" 'Twas all for your good," said Tam gently. "Billy, have ye got a seegair?"

Billy groaned and groped under the bed, produced a locked box and, with great ostentation, fumbled for and found a key which was suspended round his neck by a bootlace. With this he opened the box, took out one cigar, relocked the box and replaced it under his bed, Tam eying the proceedings without moving a muscle of his face.

"Ye can't be too careful. Billy; there's thieves about," he said as he smelled the cigar and pinched it. "Mon, what a surprise they'd get if the puir bodies burgled ye and got no better than a five-cent seegair. This is a shorter one than usual, Billy," he said after a pause, and when his challenge had provoked no comment, "they're robbin' ye."

"They are all the same size," said Billy thickly.

"Open the box again and let me compare 'em," said Tam.

"Not on yer life," said a voice which might literally be described as sweet, but which in fact sounded as though its owner were undergoing a process of slow strangulation. And for a few moments there was no sound but the scrape of Tam's pen and the indescribable noise of strong young jaws munching candy.

Then Billy asked: "What did you really say, Tam? I mean about me to Blackie."

"Ah, weel," said Tam grudgingly, "Ah said ye were no' so bad."

"And what did he say?" asked Billy eagerly.

"Weel," said Tam, "he just sneefed."

"But honestly?"

"Mon, ye're a vain pup and A'm no' going to make ye conceited."

Billy sat up suddenly on the bed. "What's that?" he asked.

"That's a Hun."

Tam lifted his head and listened.

"'Tis one of young Boelke's Frenchmen," he said.

He opened the door and stepped out, and looked upward between his shading palms.

"Come oot o' that, Billy." he shouted, and broke into a run to his hangar, but long before he reached it von Haarden was over the aerodrome.

The bomb had exploded near the headquarter office and he was wheeling backward, fighting off the guarding patrol which had closed on him.

"I'm afraid you were too late. Tam." said Blackie, standing amidst a litter of smashed glass and shattered match-boarding which had once been his clerk's office. A mechanic was running across the ground carrying a little canvas bag.

"Hello," said Blackie, "dropped a message, did he? By the way, that was von Haarden."

"A noticed it," said Tam grimly.

Blackie took the bag and opened it, read the sheet of paper it contained and grinned. By this time he had an audience, for the mess-room and quarters had emptied rapidly at the first alarm and he was surrounded by a group of officers in various stages of dishabillé.

"Listen to this!" He read:

To-day I come once. To-morrow or perhaps next day or some other time propitious I come twice and show you that it is simple for German airmen to come. I will make a bet of gloves to do this unofficially. Soldierly and fraternal greetings. von Haarden.

"Silly ass," said a disgusted voice.

"It sounds funny because his English isn't good." said Blackie, "but in reality it isn't so funny as it looks. We will watch for this fellow on the 'first day propitious.' I do not desire that he should make a merry hell of my office again."

Fighting squadrons of the Flying Corps have something more to do than to devote their attention to private vendettas. The work of the squadron is so systematized every hour of the day, every pilot and every machine is so occupied with the routine of war that the squadron can no more than reserve a corner of its collective brain for matters which are outside the official orbit.

Yet since the guarding of an aerodrome against hostile attacks is very much part of the day's work and, bet or no bet, Rittmeister von Haarden was a most formidable scout leader, Blackie detailed in the orders of the day two flights to patrol "if weather reports favorable."

Neither the next nor the following day did the enemy put in an appearance, but there was excellent reason. The weather had grown gusty, the sky was filled with low-lying clouds, and even the artillery planes were unable to go about their business.

On the afternoon of the third day the wind died down and the clouds rose with the barometer. Billy Best went up with Tam and patroled according to instructions. It was part of the unwritten law that the visit must be paid in the daytime, and it was an hour before sunset when von Haarden came along.

His arrival was signaled from the observation station two miles to the east of the aerodrome and Blackie hurried out to his telescope.

"That's not the game," he growled, and neither was it, for von Haarden was flying at something over twenty thousand feet.

Blackie looked round for the barrage flights. He counted the four machines of McAllister's flight, but Tam's four machines were invisible. Then presently he found them, and emitted a yell of exuberant joy, for Tam was also well above twenty thousand feet and his four planes were pinpoints of black in the sky and almost seemed stationary.

Tam was one of the few men who preferred the upper air. It was a saying of his that "Ye can fa' quicker than ye can climb." He was, in point of fact, a thousand feet higher than von Haarden in the region which would still be ablaze with sunshine when the sun had sunk for half an hour below the western skyline, a region so bitterly cold that even beneath his fur gloves his fingers were frozen stiff.

He saw the oncoming plane and signaled "Attack." Billy Best, who was the right of the diamond formation in which the flight was moving, dropped sheer to his quarry and got in a burst as von Haarden swung his machine to avoid the attack.

Billy saw his enemy for perhaps the tenth part of a second before he fell behind and passed the tail of the Albatross. It was just a glimpse of a man in a fur coat, his face masked, his bent head covered with a fur and leather cap, his hands gripping the joy stick.

Tam, who followed, did not see as much. Curious things happen to machine guns in the upper air. and when Tam sighted the Rittmeister his gun behaved accordingly. There is no time in air fighting to correct the mischief of a jammed gun. Before Tam could loop over and gain the height necessary for attack, the Albatross had fulfilled its mission, was crossing the aerodrome amidst a pandemonium of Archie fire and was heading due west.

Tam followed in pursuit, but he had lost too much height to reach his enemy's level and after a twenty-mile run, during which he succeeded in getting his gun working, he returned to the aerodrome.

"Hard lines, Tam," said Blackie; "go over and cheer your young Scottish friend. He's disconsolate."

Billy indeed was grieved, almost to the point of tears.

"I used to think I could shoot," he said miserably: "missed him at less than fifty yards. I was your young Nimrod all right: missed him, Tam, at fifty yards, by gosh!"

"Ah weel," said Tam philosophically, "'tis nothing to greet aboot. Maybe ye scairt him. What did ye come down for?"

"Search me!" said the wretched Billy. "I just felt lonely and homesick."

"Get up," said the stern Tam. "Up wi' ye, ye whining little deevil. Is it no' twice the laddie is coming."

Tam took another machine, tested the gun and rose with Billy to join the flight. He had reached the high level when a Lucas lamp flickered from the aerodrome.

Tam read the message: "Von Haarden coming back. Get him this time."

For ten minutes Tam searched the heavens in vain and presently he saw the big Albatross. It was flying much lower and again was heading straight for the aerodrome. Tam shot off three rounds from his gun and then thought of Billy.

Billy should have his chance. He signaled "Nearest attack," and Billy swept down the six thousand feet which separated him from his enemy. Tam watched the planes growing nearer and nearer, saw Billy turn on a parallel course with the Albatross.

The boy might make sure but it was a terribly dangerous position to take. Closer and closer the planes approached one another. Billy would be waiting for von Haarden to show himself, and Tam watched as he dropped in a wide circle toward the two machines. And then an amazing thing happened. The Albatross and Billy's scout were running almost side by side, and less than fifty yards separated them and nothing happened.

As Tam looked, he saw Billy bank over and turn, leaving the Albatross to pursue its course over the aerodrome. Almost immediately Blackie signaled "Flight return."

When Tam reached the ground Billy was standing before Blackie.

"Well, Best," said Blackie, "I'm afraid von Haarden's won his bet."

"Yes, sir," said Billy simply.

"Did your gun jam?" asked Blackie.

"Did ye no' fire?" Tam interrupted anxiously.

"No, sir," said Billy. "I didn't fire and my gun didn't jam."

"For God's sake, what happened then?"

"I don't understand it, sir," said Billy, and his face was white. "It was awful. It can't possibly have happened. I saw von Haarden as plainly as I see you —"

"And?" asked Blackie.

"He was dead, sir. He had been dead an hour," said Billy.

An hour later a German Albatross crashed within a hundred yards of the aerodrome. It crashed because its petrol had run out. For two hours it had been moving in a wide circle that carried it from Mossy Face Wood to the aerodrome across the back areas, round to the wood again and again back to the aerodrome. It had been moving steadily, unswervingly, just so long as its petrol lasted, with a dead man's stiff hand at its control—for Billy had killed him with his first shot.

"It's a verra moot point," said Tam to Billy that night as he sat on the edge of his bed smoking a cigar luxuriously, "whether that puir body, Mad Haarden, won his bet. Speakin' theologically I think he did. and A'm goin' over Mossy Face Wood tomorrow to drop a pair of yeer gloves."

"Why my gloves?" demanded Billy truculently.

CHAPTER VI

THE DÉBUT OF WILLIAM BEST

There is a loneliness more poignant than that "loneliness of wings" of which Leonardo wrote; there is the loneliness of anonymity. To be one of twenty thousand men or more, roughly classified heroic by an admiring but misunderstanding public, is to endure the same crushing sense of obliteration which comes to all men in a crowd.

Billy Best realized fully enough that he was a member of a great and wonderful brotherhood. It was a brotherhood which included in its membership even those men who daily sought his destruction in the air and whom he variously described, according to his mood, as Fritz, Heinie, Boche, Hun, Jerry, or "them."

For Billy had adopted the nomenclature of both armies, French and British. There had been a time when he had thought that it was low down that terms of contempt should be employed against German fighting men who were undoubtedly brave, who were certainly patriotic and who, whatever might be the justice of their cause, were entitled to respect.

But he had learned in the great school of war that such phrases were not contemptuous, but were rather labels applied by high-spirited young men to a foe whose valor they respected but of whose inferiority to themselves they were perfectly convinced.

Billy lived among men whose names, if they did not reach the newspaper-press—for the British government was a little too conservative on the publicity side of the war—were familiarly spoken of in every mess-room he visited. He learned of the little feuds between particular French and British squadrons and particular German squadrons. He knew why von Heuben went regularly to a certain aerodrome behind Rheims looking for Villiers, the French ace, and why Villiers avoided meeting the man who was his half-brother.

He knew why the Captain Baron von Kohn was killed by Seveni, the Italian airman in circumstances so remarkable that one hesitates to record them, since the two men had fought a duel behind a German aerodrome under the eyes of a princely army commander. And von Kohn's offense had been so great in the eyes of honorable men that Seveni, after killing his man, was allowed to go back to his machine which stood in the center of the German ground and retire unmolested.

He knew of "Eighteen" Spanton, so called because on his eighteenth birthday, which was the eighteenth of the month, he shot down his eighteenth enemy plane and died that night in number eighteen general hospital. He knew of the men in the German service that both the French and British knew, of Boelke, Immelmann, and the two Richthofens and their kind, and he knew also that in the German messes there were French and British fighters who were discussed at every table.

Had not Tam been challenged by three or four of the most famous of fighters? Had not Blackie been signaled out by Bissing's circus in the old days?

All these men knew one another though they had never met. Their methods, their character, their systems of fighting were discussed and criticized in very much the same way as the form of a race-horse or of a team player is discussed by the votaries of sport. And he was of the crowd, one of the unmentioned, and it depressed him, not because he was a lover of the spot- light, not because he was looking forward to seeing his name figure in the world's press, but rather from a mistaken sense of his unworthiness.

He was piqued with the feeling that he did not count. With youth happily such moments of depression are of brief duration, but while they last there is no denying that they are fairly intensive.

"Ye ought to be ashamed of yersel'," said Tam severely. "A'm surprised at ye, Billy."

"Oh, shut up," said Billy, a sad figure in shirt-sleeves sitting in the one chair of which Tam's modest apartment boasted, his elbows on his knees, his face in his hands. "I just feel out of it; I'll never make a scout."

"Will ye be quiet," said Tam; "have ye no candy to put in yeer face, and after me teachin' ye the art and science of scootin'? Have ye no sense of decency or will ye be an American to the end of yeer days?"

"I guess there's nothing wrong with America," said Billy, reviving sufficiently to defend his native land against the aspersions of a foreigner. "It's me that's wrong."

"What would ye like?" demanded Tam, sitting on the edge of the table and eying the other with disfavor. "Would ye like me to put a wee bit in the Glasgow Herald, or maybe ye'd like to see yeer portrait in the police news?"

"Forget all that," said Billy rudely; "you know that doesn't cut any ice with me. I'm just no good. Do you know what happened to-day?"

"A'm waitin' to learn." said Tam; "all this afternoon A've been sitting by patiently and, if A may use the word, modestly, waitin' for yeer confession. Ye've done something, Billy. A can see it in yeer fairtive glances. Yeer color comes and goes. Yeer hands shake like a brigade movie. Yeer breath is labored. Ye wear a hunted and a haunted look. Tell me the worst, laddie. Have yeer parents no' sent the candy they promised ye?"

Billy snarled something rude.

"Oot wi' it," said Tam.

The boy rose to his feet and thrust his hands deep into the pockets of his slacks.

"Tam," he said and then there was a long silence which Tam did not break. "I just hate to tell you;" then quickly, "Did you hear anything to-day—about me, I mean?"

"A haird ye were pursood by Mr. Mac Bissing and his world-renowned caircus!"

"That's right," said Billy and his face was long and glum. "Tam—gee! I was scared sick! It came over me all in a moment. My mouth went dry and my hands shook and all my bones seemed to turn to water. What do you think of that?"

A bright and kindly light dawned in Tam's eyes. "A'm glad ye told me," he said quickly, "and A'm glad it's ower."

"Over? What do you mean?"

Tam slid down to the floor and laid his hand on the boy's shoulder. "Billy," he said, "d'ye think, that A've no' had that feelin'?"

"You? Why, of course you haven't."

"Mon, I had it to-day," said Tam. "A have it regularly twice a week. A never see a Hun maneuvering for ma tail withoot A don't wish A were home suppin' tea wi' ma Aunt Elizabeth. I have no Aunt Elizabeth, but A often, wish A had. If ye went to Blackie and told him, he would tell ye the same. If ye had a heart-to-heart talk with Richthofen, he would tell ye the same. If ye went down to the Frenchies' aerodrome and talked it over with the aces, they would all tell ye the same. They're scared to death. If it wasn't for that, air fighting would be wilful murder. As it is, it is just justifiable homicide in self-defense."

"But do you mean," demanded Billy, "that feeling like that I am fit for scouting—that I'll have those sensations again?"

"If ye're normal ye will," said Tam; "if ye're mad ye won't. It's a sign ye're healthy, Billy. It relieves ma mind. A was afraid ye were smoking too much."

"Do you really mean that?" said Billy brightening up.

"A mean it," said Tam, and his sincerity carried conviction.

Billy remembered this conversation the next morning when forming one of the escort to a bombing squadron which was making its way toward a much too active railway junction, he found himself engaged with that very circus which had occasioned him so much misgiving.

It cheered him to feel that his sensations had their counterpart in the bosom of an invisible German pilot who at that moment was firing at him through his propeller, and when he maneuvered to his enemy's tail and, following him down in a nose dive, saw the German machine crash and burst into flames, he experienced the righteous sense of satisfaction which comes to the respectable householder who has got the first shot at an armed burglar.

What Tam had not told Billy was that no airman succeeds until he has evolved a system of his own and developed characteristics which remove him from the general run of good workmen and place him in a class by himself. Such things are not to be told to the young lest they form "ground theories," for systems of fighting are born in a flash in moments of deadly crises. They can not be worked out by rote nor puzzled out in leisure moments.

The versification of air fighting may be mechanically mastered, its poetry defies research and comes in that second of inspiration when the soul of the man who acquires the knowledge is trembling on the brink of eternity.

Billy did things according to the book. He knew all the tricks that skilled masters could teach him, did as well, in fact, as any other good man who had a hand light enough to manipulate the controls of a fast and sensitive scout. He knew when to sideslip, when to loop, when to fall into a tail dive. He knew how to dodge shrapnel and when it need not be dodged. He understood the mechanical side of reconnaissance. In fact, he was, as so many other men have been, a credit to the masters who had pumped into his receptive mind the a-b-c of his work.

It was all to his advantage that he was consumed with that divine discontent which is the very hallmark of genius and that he could detect between his own methods and those of his compeers a difference so subtle as to evade him.

The men of the Flying Corps have no secrets from one another. Their systems are individual and, giving their frankness its lowest value, there is nothing to be gained by preserving a reticence about a method which, since no two men think and act alike, is inimitable.

Bradbury, the American ace, came over to the Umpty-fourth and to him as a compatriot Billy opened his heart. Bradbury listened without smiling.

"There's nothing to it," he said when Billy had finished; "it's just adapting the know-how in a novel way that makes the star airman, I guess—it will come to you. After you've crashed about a dozen Germans you'll find the way you can crash 'em best and then you'll be a specialist."

"Huh!" said Billy without enthusiasm.

There was little opportunity for specialism during the ensuing days and nights. Early morning reconnaissance work, escort duty to bombing squadrons, patrol guard over the artillery planes, these and other duties of a similar kind offer little scope for the display of initiative.

Billy had a fight or two with "sausage killers," those venomous wasps who shoot their fiery sting at the helpless and obese observation balloons. He interfered with the comfort of a too venturesome enemy patrol. He enjoyed a little fight on his own over the Lille aerodrome (his enemy was obviously a novice and dived for safety after the first burst of fire) and he experienced the discomforts attendant upon a crash of his own.

Then one day his opportunity came. He was one of a flight told off to escort a special train running from Calais to Paris conveying some important members of the British Government to an inter-allied conference. His flight had to cover eighty miles of the journey where the escort duty was taken up by another flight. Nothing untoward occurred and the train was formally handed over to the new escort and the flight had turned northward on its homeward journey when far away to the right and flying at a considerable elevation Billy saw a solitary airplane which from its shape he judged was German. Tam's sharp eyes had seen the machine and he had no doubt. He signaled Billy to investigate and Billy swung off eastward. It was indubitably an enemy plane. What was its mission, why it was so far behind the lines or how it had evaded the patrols, Billy did not trouble to think.

At any rate, the enemy machine was not evading Billy and it came round and began a swift glide in his direction. It was an Albatross scout, obviously a two-gun machine, and Billy maneuvered to avoid unpleasantness, recognizing with dismay the certain symptoms of approaching panic. Despite the encouraging talk he had had with Tam those symptoms developed alarmingly.

He felt his breath coming in short gasps. He had a curious sensation in the pit of his stomach. He felt himself breaking into a perspiration and cursed.

The hand at the gun was steady enough. He would have only the fraction of a second to meet and counter the attack. He was horribly lonely and then suddenly his fear turned to an almost insane anger. Why should this man wish to destroy him? What had he done to deserve—

Zip! Zip! Zip!

He felt the bullets whistle past him and saw a great rent in the canvas of his wings. A strut snapped and a wire hung loose. All this he saw before the attacking Albatross flashed by.

Billy banked over in a cold rage and dived straight for the machine. He had no other desire but to ram his enemy.

In the second of time between taking his decision and swooping down to carry it into effect he felt a wild exaltation at the thought of the smash which was coming when the full weight of his heavy scout traveling at one hundred and twenty miles an hour struck home. He had bloody murder in his heart, and only by a miracle did the Albatross escape. Down went the nose of the German, Billy on his tail. By this time something of the old training had asserted itself. He reached for his gun and emptied a tray of ammunition at the falling machine. Something jumped out of the wing, something that looked like a stick with a piece of rag attached. Billy fired again and this time with deadly effect. The machine was wrapped in a pall of smoke, pierced by long streamers of flame.

Cadet William Best returned to the aerodrome of the Umpty-fourth in a condition bordering upon the ecstatic. He strutted over to Tam and clapped him on the shoulder with gross familiarity. "Son," he said, "I've found it!"

Tam looked up guiltily. "A've found it mesel'," he said; "'twas under yeer pillow. Mon, those seegairs of yours are no' what they're cracked up to be."

"I don't mean the key of my box, you pirate," chortled Billy; "I've found my métier."

"Oh aye," said Tam, "she'll be a bonny lass, but ye're ower young to think o' marryin'."

"Métier!" roared Billy. "I'm the Terror of the Skies."

"Ye'll have to fight me for that championship," said Tam. "What's the sky been doin' to ye?"

"I am the rammer," said Billy, biting off the end of a large cigar.

"Open the window," begged Tam; "it's the sun, Billy. Ye'll feel all right in a minute. What have ye been ramming?"

Not briefly did Billy relate his story. He told it in detail. He gave sectional views of his emotions. He described how he felt and why he felt it.

"Condensin' yeer serial story," said Tam after a very patient hearing, "into a few pithy paragraphs, A gather ye made an attempt to damage government property and commit suicide and that the heat of yeer language and the fire in yeer eye set a light to puir wee Fritzie. Have ye any other statement to make before A report the disgusting caircumstances to yeer superior officer?"

"But wasn't it fine, Tam?"

"A'm no' so sure," said the cautious Tam, "and at the same time A'm no' so sure it wasn't. If yeer daring exploit was witnessed by the other Fritzies ye'll have a reputation for insanity which ought to make yeer fortune."

Billy's reputation came in a night, was consolidated in a week. His system was a simple one. It was no more and no less than a series of desperate attempts on his part to collide with enemy airplanes. Had he succeeded he would not have survived his success. The story of how he fell spread-eagle upon the great von Bissing and of how that gentleman, one of the most skilful ot fighters, did not look back until he reached his aerodrome; the story of his head-on dive at Major von Hoffer; the story of his gallant attempt to ram von Richthofen himself, have been told so often and have been exaggerated and embellished so frequently that it is not necessary to describe all the particulars of those remarkable combats.

At the end of the second week German airmen prisoners brought the news that several expert fighters were looking for the "mad dog" and Billy was in the seventh heaven of delight. Nobody checked him, because that is not the way of the air service. Nobody warned him or counseled moderation. Battles are not won by paying heed to such counsel. They gave him the best and the fastest machine they could find and they said good-by to him every time he went out, without any great hope that he would be back to lunch.

Tam, whose methods had more finesse, watched his jubilant subordinate and on one occasion, at least, relieved Billy of responsibility by driving down the machine which the boy was maneuvering to crash.

The moral effect upon the enemy was great. Even the skilled fighters gave him a wide berth. Elkstein, who was shot down behind the British lines, explained this reluctance to face the bull-rush dive of the "Rammer."

"It is good to be killed by fair shooting, also by clever maneuverment, but it is like to be knocked down in the street by a beer wagon for a gallant soldier to outgo from life in such brutal circumstances."

And Billy reigned supreme, the joy of a hundred tiny mess-rooms up and down the line, until the day that Lieutenant Heinrich Mickelbaum went up in an old-type Taube escorted by a fighting squadron of German scouts and sought the Rammer in that sky area where he loved to roam.

The Intelligence Department of the Royal Flying Corps is singularly efficient. It works in conjunction with other Intelligence Departments and the news it secures is both curious and accurate.

On the morning when Lieutenant Heinrich Mickelbaum and his escort rose, Tam. who had been on an early morning flight, came into the room where Billy was shaving.

"Billy," said he, "A want to see ye."

"Feast yer eyes," said Billy arrogantly.

"'Tis not so fillin'," said Tam; "mon. will ye never lairn that it is ridiculous to put a reaper over asphalt? A had a dream aboot ye last night."

"You don't say?" said Billy politely.

"A dreamt A was making up a bit of poetry about ye, Billy, and was writing a letter to yeer misguided parents. 'Dear father and mother of Billy Best,' writes I, 'yeer puir foolish son is no more. We shall miss him, but the Hun did not, so no more at present. From his late—but never too late to learn—friend. Tam.'"

"Ah," said Billy, fingering his chin with satisfaction.

"The point of ma story is to come." said Tam. "Billy, the authorities are worried about ye and they have got a graund stunt for ye. A've come to bring the news."

Billy looked round anxiously. "What's wrong, Tam?"

"Let other lips tell ye," said Tam. shaking his head; "A hate to bring ye the sad news, but they're trying to save yeer life It seems unnecessary, but ye must humor the foolish people."

"What's the joke?" demanded Billy.

"Whether 'twas a telegram from President Wilson or Doctor Wilson, as the case may be, or whether they want ye for the movies noo that Charlie Chapiin's joining up, or whether the Gairman Emperor has threatened reprisals, A don't know."

The mystery was cleared up when Billy put in his appearance at the orderly room and was introduced to a quiet-looking gentleman in the uniform of a staff-major who proved to be Sir George Cannel, the aeronautical expert.

"This is Mr. Best, sir," said Major Blackie.

The staff-officer nodded. "We have reason to believe that the Hun is going to get you, Mr. Best." he said, "and as we are anxious not to lose you, we thought that we would like to make a sporting experiment which might or might not save your life and which might or might not prove that certain of our theories are right."

"Yes, sir," said Billy, groping for light.

The officer took up a fairly large bundle which lay across Blackie's desk. It looked like a tightly rolled blanket, though the material was of a much finer texture. Protruding from one end of the bundle were a number of straps.

"This is the Cannel parachute." he smiled; "it is, in fact, my own invention. We have had one or two experiments from airplanes, but they have not been wholly successful and we have never tried them out in fighting airplanes. Your peculiar method of fighting, however, enables us to —er—er—"

"Make the experiment on my foul body," smiled Billy; "yes, sir, I would be very pleased."

"I would not guarantee," said the staff-officer, "that this is going to save your life, but that doesn't seem to matter much."

"Not at all, sir," said Billy cheerfully.

"I beg your pardon," laughed the major; "what I mean is that if you collide in midair without this, you are certainly killed. With this you have a fifty to fifty chance of escaping."

Billy hesitated. "Is that exactly fair to the other man, sir?" he asked.

"The German?"

Billy nodded.

"I shouldn't worry very much about him," said the officer dryly; "it is by no means a certainty that you will escape. The odds are two to one that the parachute will get entangled in the fuselage. It is not like a clean drop from a balloon. It is an even chance that you will be insensible when the crash comes and be unable to operate. In fact, the, chances are all against you."

"I'll take 'em then," said Billy promptly.

The necessary instructions did not take very long. The working of the parachute was simplicity itself, always providing he could jump clear of the falling machine. If it turned turtle or fell sideways the chances of saving his life were remote.

Billy, strapped and belted, with the parachute lightly fastened to the nacelle behind him and the release string within his reach, went up in search of adventure with less pleasure than he usually experienced when he set forth. Adventure he soon found and that immediately behind the German line. Six enemy machines, five of the newest pattern and one which was strange to him and which was obviously slower than the rest, came into sight and then, as if on some signal, four of the six retired, leaving a slow monoplane to meet the Rammer.

Billy maneuvered for height and reached his enemy's level. He did not doubt that the usual thing would happen, that before his devastating rush his enemy would drop in flight, exposing himself to the pursuer's gun.

Something within him made him hesitate to attack. It wasn't fair. The chances were not equal. If he were sure that the parachute would not act, he would have gone joyously to the fight; but there was an outside risk of safety. His opponent settled all misgivings by suddenly turning and heading his way. In a moment Billy forgot his scruples. Straight at the Taube he went, all out, his engines roaring like a mill. Nearer and nearer—then Billy realized with a gasp and a return of the old panic feeling that the machine would not avoid him. This, then, was Billy's last fight. He recognized its inevitability, saw the end and with a quick jerk of his hand released the safety-catch of the parachute.

The machines collided at an angle. Billy leaped up into the air and was jerked back by the weight of the parachute. He was horribly shocked and jarred. He did not know what had happened to the machines save that they had collided. He smelled something burning, was flung upward again and was again pulled back and felt himself falling, falling at a terrifying rate through the air.

He closed his eyes. "He did not pray nor experience the slightest tinge of fear. He was just curious and found himself wondering why there was such pressure under his arms. He opened his eyes and looked up. Above his head was spread a big circular umbrella shape. The parachute had acted.

He almost fainted for the first time in his life as he realized the fact. He looked down. He saw the two machines whirling downward in smoke and flame, tumbling (slowly as it seemed) to earth and again felt that twinge of remorse that he had experienced before the fight had started.

"Poor devil," he muttered, "it wasn't fair."

Somebody was talking, yelling is a better word, cursing would be a truer description. With an effort he turned round. Not fifty yards away and level with him was another parachute and suspended therefrom a red-faced German officer who alternately cursed him in English and German.

"Pig! Schweinehund!" he roared. "You have no bravery. Ha! You have parachute. You can not take risk. You always have parachute, you brave fellow."

"You're a liar!" veiled Billy.

"Pig!" said the German.

"When I get down I'll break your head!" shouted Billy.

The parachutes were drifting nearer together. Conversation was almost impossible unless the men raised their voices.

"You are so bold a fellow that you can not come up to fight mit German gentleman mitout a parachute, eh?"

"Listen, you poor boob," yelled Billy; "what do you think you are hanging on to, a damned Christmas-tree?"

They were still quarreling violently when they descended gently into a field behind the British support line. They were quarreling when delighted Tommies released them from their straps and from the staff car that carried them both back to headquarters. The sound of their recriminations came to the admiring soldiery long after they had passed out of sight round the bend of the road.

CHAPTER VII

THE CLOUD FISHERS

"Are you going through Bézierville, Tam?"

"Aye an' no," replied Tam cautiously.

"What in thunder do you mean?" asked Major Blackie irritably. "Either you're going or not going!"

"Well, sir," said Tam. "A'm goin' to Bézierville to buy a few cheap seegairs, 'tis Mr. Baxter's bairthday to-morrow an' A thocht A'd gi'e him a surprise, the puir body. A'm no' goin' through Bézierville—but intae Bézierville."

Blackie laughed and picked up a heavy leather case from his desk.

"You're a long-winded beggar," he said. "Drop these at Advance Survey—they're photographic plates which young Oathwaite exposed on his last reconnaissance. Get a receipt from the photographic gentleman—be careful as to this; photographs have been going astray lately and G.H.Q. has been kicking up the devil of a shine."

Tam took the leathern wallet, received the printed receipt-form and passed out to the motor-cycle and side-car. He tucked the plates carefully away in the bottom of the little carriage and pushed off.

Bézierville (this is not the real name of the town) lies twenty-three miles due southwest of the Umpty-fourth's aerodrome, and as the Advance Survey Office lies half a mile west of the town, the journey certainly involved a change in Tam's original plan, since it was necessary to pass through the narrow streets of the town and emerge through the mossy bastions of what had once been Bézierville's western gate. He entered the gaunt dwelling-house where the Survey had its headquarters and found the slim, spectacled chief of the development department.

"Umpty-fourth Squadron—Wytschaete Sector—h'm," said the young man, reading the label. "Why are they photographing that part of the line?"

Tam liked or disliked people very quickly. He instantly decided that he disliked this young man very much indeed.

"It's no' for me to tell ye," he said; "but mebbe it's grawin' auld; or grawin' whiskers; or mebbe the Commander-in-Chief wants to frame it an' hang it o'er his bed."

The young man looked at him sharply. He was a civilian and apparently recognized no urgent reason why he should be polite to a junior lieutenant.

"You're a humorist." he said. "Yes?"

Tam shook his head. "Not so ye'd notice it," he said, and added as an afterthought, "Mister Lavinski."

The young man went red. "Look here," he said loudly, "you mustn't get fresh with me because you're an officer, you know. My name isn't Lavinski—see? I'm not here to be insulted, and I shall report you to the G. O. C."

"Oh, aye," said Tam with approval, "mention ma name to him—'tis one he'll remember."

"I've no wish to hold any further conversation with you," said the photographer loftily and turned away.

"Here! Come back, ma impetuous laddie, an' gi'e me ye'r autograph on this bit receipt. It will sairve as a souveneer," he said as the other hastily scrawled his signature.

Tam blotted and folded the receipt and moved leisurely from the office. He was mounting his bicycle when the young man appeared at the doorway and, after a few seconds hesitation, came down to the scout.

"Excuse me if I got a bit heated up," he said; "it's very worrying work. My name's Yeldstein—Dutch, but lived all my life in dear old Blighty. Grand country, England."

"So A've heard." said Tam gravely; "'tis the wild land sooth of Glasgae, A'm told, but I have never explored it."

"Oh, you are Scotch."

"Scots," corrected Tam.

"A grand country, Scotland," said Mr. Yeldstein. "Maybe you know my two cousins. They've got a store in Perth—MacPherson Brothers. Ike's a good chap, so's Abe."

"A never mix with the hieland nobility," said Tam.

"Look here, Mr. What's-yer-name," Mr. Yeldstein went on. "I hope we are not going to be bad friends."

"It's no use hopin'," said Tam solemnly.

"Any time you're around this way, look me up. I've got quarters here," he pointed to a large barn-like building behind the house, "you will always find a drop of the real wine of Scotland—you know what I mean."

"Aye," said Tam, wilfully dense, "ginger ale."

He would have made a dignified retirement, but his front tire just at that moment decided to go "phut!" and Mr. Yeldstein became the soul of hospitality, summoning slaves from dark rooms and workshops to repair the damage, and carrying the unwilling Tam to his quarters.

The place had originally been a storehouse, but its new owner's native genius had transformed it into a very comfortable living-room. The dark young man produced whisky and large and opulent-looking cigars with imposing gold bands.

"Just make yourself comfortable," he said, "while I run over to the office and tell my people where I am. We are getting photographs every hour of the day and night." He called back from the doorway, "You will find the soda in that second cupboard."

Tam was not very keen on drinking, but he had his ideas as to what was and what was not polite. There were two doors, but the first did not reveal either a cupboard or a wine-store. It was, in fact, the entrance to a small room innocent of anything more refreshing than might be contained in six large steel cylinders.

Tam was peering into the interior in his quest for soda siphons when Mr. Yeldstein returned.

"No, not there!" said the photographer hastily; "the next!"

He shut the door hurriedly, slipped a key from his pocket and locked it, and Tam noticed that his face was very red.

"Some photographic stuff. I thought the da—I thought the bally room was locked."

Tam found the soda, refreshed himself and took farewell of his voluble host, who, from the moment of his return to the room to the moment he shook hands with unnecessary heartiness, did not stop speaking.

Tam mentioned the matter casually to Blackie the next day.

"He is a pretty useful photographer, I believe, and was in a good way of business in the north of England when he was called up," said Blackie.

"A'm no' so sure that A like him," said Tam; "ye were tellin' me, Major Blackie, sir, that photographs of the lines have been going astray."

Blackie nodded.

"We have found several very confidential maps in the German lines when we raided them," said Blackie; "there has been an awful row about it, but obviously they must have come through some neutral country."

"It's verra likely," said Tam; "then again it's verra unlikely."

Blackie groaned. "I can see you joining the Intelligence Department," he said.

A week later Tam took a flight to escort a dozen bombing machines on a night raid.

It was one of those commonplace affairs which ordinarily receive a line such as, "bombs were dropped on enemy dumps." in the official communiqué, and the escort had a simple and uneventful time, turning in the direction of their headquarters soon after midnight. In order to facilitate their return, the raiders followed the course of a little river which carried them west and south of their homes, turning north again when the lights of Bézierville showed on their right. This brought the raiders immediately over Bézierville, to which they had signaled their innocent character in order that the civilians of that town should endure no agony of mind.

Tam, leading the squadron, had crossed the dull silver thread which marked the river south of the town, when something big and soft struck the nose of his machine, was jerked violently backward by the tractor, and hit the little pilot full in the face.

He flung out his hand and pushed the thing away and it disappeared, leaving on his knees a thin cotton bag some ten inches square and torn at the neck, as he subsequently discovered.

The occurrence was alarming, though from first to last it had occupied less than a second of time. Tam turned in his seat and flashed from his Lucas lamp an anxious inquiry to the following squadron. Sixteen lamps winked O. K. and Tam went on, mystified.

Blackie chuckled when Tam recounted the mysterious appearance.

"You were quite unconsciously sailing under an enemy squadron," he said. "They were reported in the region of Bézierville at ten o'clock. Probably one of the pilots dropped something overboard. You ought to be thankful it wasn't anything worse."

"Oh," said Tom, relieved, "is that a'? They bombed Bézierville A've nae doot."

"No," said Blackie. "They did not drop anything on that little dorp, so far as I can find out. As a matter of fact, they are rather keen on Bézierville, though what they expect to find there, Heaven knows. There is always a Hun scout or two in that region, but they usually choose daybreak for their reconnaissance."

Tam scratched his chin. "That's verra strange," he said.

This was in the early hours of Tuesday morning. An hour before dawn on the Wednesday, Tam left the aerodrome, flying his tiny Hepworth Kitten and headed straight for Bézierville. He awaited the dawn and beyond the dawn and saw nothing. The next morning he repeated his visit, this time flying at an incredible height, and had the satisfaction of watching three very fast German machines come swiftly from the east, circle widely about Bézierville in the very first light of dawn and return to their bases. He did not attack them then nor the following morning when, through his glasses, he witnessed something which left him gasping.

"They waire machines of the Intelligence Squad." he reported, "and Major Blackie, sir, the Gairmans have a grand stoont."

What that stunt was he described in detail, and it was Blackie's turn to gasp. Tam made a personal report to the corps commander, and that gray veteran listened in absorbed silence.

"It seems incredible," he said, "and yet it can be only that. We know maps are getting across to the other side, but as to how they manage it, the Intelligence are in the dark. Take all the men you want from any of the squadrons, Major Blackie," he said, turning to the squadron commander, "and see what you can do in the morning."

The next scene of the drama was set on a bleak road where an anti-aircraft waited patiently for the dawn.

The battery commander scanned the heavens through his glasses—carefully covering that gray patch of sky which represented his "area of protection." His signaler lay face downward by the side of the dusty road, a telephone receiver clamped to his ears, and carried on a sotto voce conversation with a young gentleman similarly employed at a distant observation post.

Now and again he raised his official voice to convey military secrets:

"Passin' Q. B. 73 T. sir—headin' for Q. Y. 99 B., sir."

The battery threw a glance left and right to the big trolleys where the A. A. guns pointed their slim noses upward; to the expectant gun-crews, their faces turned to the officer at the range-finder, then returned to the inspection of the clouded blue.

Suddenly: "Swat that fly!" A monotonous voice drawled range and deflection.

"Bang! Bang! Bang!"

The Archies flashed and roared. Black smudges of smoke and white puff-balls appeared against the clouds, and through it all sailed one serene bird, dazzling white and almost ethereal in the dawn light.

The intruder into these forbidden realms neither swerved to the right nor to the left. The impression left on the mind of the observer was that the pilot was unconscious of the discourteous greeting. Shells burst beneath, above, before, behind, but this swift dragon-fly hummed on its course and presently was out of range of this anti-aircraft battery on the road and was receiving the attention of another Archie group three miles to the westward.

The battery commander ordered "Cease Fire," and walked across to his second in command.

"Fritz is in a hurry—reconnaissance?"

His captain was drinking from the cup of a vacuum flask and shook his head.

"Solitary Fritzes hardly go on reconnaissance work," he said; "he's carrying a message to one of our aerodromes and—"

"Passin' due north Lorette headin' for Q Y. 99 B., sir," yelled the signaler.

"Stand by!"

Again the white-winged dragon-fly came streaking through the air—eastward this time. Again the Archies banged and crashed and the trollies jerked and swayed to and fro with every explosion, as a tiny boat oscillates in the wash of a passing steamer.

"Cease fire!" The battery commander walked over to his second, filling his pipe. "That fellow was nearer fifteen thousand than ten thousand," he growled.

"Twelve thousand and four hundred, sir," replied the other; "he didn't stay long—that's one of ours following." He pointed eastward.

Another plane was in the skies—the snarl of her engines came to them above the ceaseless pulsation of the distant guns. It was climbing as it progressed, climbing perceptibly.

"That fellow's moving some—a fast scouting-machine." said the battery commander.

The machine banked over suddenly and began to climb in big spirals. Higher and higher it climbed till it reached that altitude where even the rising sun failed to find reflection on its wings and it became a black speck. The artillerymen watched the climb for ten minutes before a new diversion came. It was afforded by the appearance in the east of a big formation which went slowly across the sky at an altitude of twelve thousand feet.

"Twenty-five—twenty-six—twenty-seven—say thirty," counted the gunner officer.

"Thirty-two," suggested his companion, "or thirty-three, counting the watcher up aloft—I wonder what the devil he's doing up there?"

"Passin' Q. B. 73 T., sir—headin' for Q. Y. 99 B., sir," rasped the weary signaler on the ground.

It was the white German returning; the gunners recognized her. She was following a course identical with that which she had pursued less than half an hour before. Again she winged her contemptuous way through the shrapnel which a western battery was flinging at her.

"'Old fire against 'ostile aircraft approachin' Q. Y.99 B., sir," sang the signaler.

"Here comes the watcher!" said the battery commander as the speck in the sky grew larger and larger.

"Ticka licka tickal"

The chatter of the machine-gun came to the men on the road—then something in the long white "body" of the enemy burst into flame and the machine dropped sideways and tail down to the earth, the "watcher" swooping down in his tracks.

"He ought to fall somewhere about here," speculated the battery commander. "What a devil of a time it takes to get 'em down—here she comes!"

Come "she" did, with a thud and jangle on the very center of the white road a hundred yards away.

The gunners started at a run for the blazing wreckage, the battery commander himself leading the way and dashing through the evil-smelling smoke to the very heart of the blaze; his scorched hands wrenched away the strap which fastened the pilot to his seat and lifted him out.

He was unconscious and bleeding from the neck, but there was no appearance of any fatal wound. The big gunner carried the insensible man a dozen yards and laid him on the side of the road. His face was black with smoke, his fair hair was singed and amber brown.

"A good-looking fellow for a Fritz," said the battery commander, scientifically bandaging the neck wound, which was apparently superficial. "Open his tunic, Grey. Ah! Nothing wrong there. I suppose the poor devil got it when he crashed."

He filled a cup with hot coffee from his vacuum flask and forced open the airman's teeth.

"Drink hearty, Fritzie," he said.

The eyelids of the prostrate man fluttered, he gasped and choked and muttered something in German. His destroyer had landed in a near-by field and the pilot had descended and was walking rapidly toward the group, shedding his gloves as he came.

First he made his way to the blazing machine, hopping in and out of the spluttering fire till at last he emerged with a long bamboo pole to the end of which was fastened a thin, steel grapnel-hook. He laid this down by the side of the road carefully and walked toward the circle of men about the fallen airman.

"Your bird, I think," said the battery commander.

"Aye," said the pilot.

He stooped down, unfastened the remaining buttons of the German's tunic and felt gingerly into first one and then the other of the inside pockets. From the latter he took a flat case of limp leather and opened it, disclosing a map which was protected by a mica covering. He nodded and grinned and carefully transferred the case to his own pocket.

Now, it was not unusual for a pilot to carry a map. Ordinarily that map is so disposed in his machine that there is no difficulty about its consultation. It is on the other hand, very unusual for a map to be carried in a pocket which is wholly unget-at-able, and it was more unusual still that a German airman prisoner, awakening to consciousness, should signify that his first thought was of a map which obviously he could not be employing for the purpose of his flight.

The young man, still dazed, his eyes half closed, stirred uneasily and spoke again in the same muttering tone. Then his hands felt for his inside pocket. For a moment he explored and then with a curse he sat bolt upright, staring from face to face. It took him some little time to grasp his unfortunate position and to realize that he was not among friends.

"How did you know?" he asked in English, and he addressed the little Scottish aviator who was standing over him regarding him with a look in which solicitude and amusement were blended.

"A've second sight," said the other solemnly; "'tis a failure o' mine."

The man on the ground groaned and closed his eyes and presently he spoke again.

"I think I can get up now."

"You had better remain where you are." said the battery commander, and Tam nodded.

"We're gettin' our electroplated limousine for ye," he said with a note of sarcasm in his tone; "'tis not often we meet the like o' ye."

All this was very mysterious to the battery commander, but he was too old a soldier to ask questions.

Presently the "electroplated limousine" came up in a cloud of dust, and proved to be a very grimy staff car into which the shaken young man was assisted.

Tam picked up the bamboo pole and strapped it to his nacelle, started up his engine and, flying at a thousand feet, overtook and passed his prisoner and was waiting for him in the aerodrome when the car pulled up before Squadron Headquarters.

The formality of checking the name and division of the prisoner, of asking him the conventional questions which he as conventionally refused to answer, was got through and Tam and his commander were alone in the office.

"Now let us have a look at that map," said Blackie.

Tam took the case from his pocket and opened it on the table. It was a very ordinary photographic map, what is termed a mosaic, that is to say it was made up of a number of squares which had been accurately photographed by airmen and pieced together, and, unlike most mosaics, it was small, the squares being little more than an inch either way.

"How did you get him?" asked Blackie, looking up.

Tam coughed. "It's no' for me," he said modestly, "to speak in praise o' ma own foresight an' acumen."

"Well don't," said Blackie.

"On the ither hand," Tam continued, "'twould be doing a grave injustice to the Umpty-fourth if I were to mask ma light. At 5:26 on the mornin' of the 4th instant A received a communication from ma respected commander to the effect that hostile aircraft of seenister design, to wit the Gairman Intelligence Department, had been behavin' strangely and even insultingly—"

"Now, Tam, cut all that," said Blackie; "I sent you out to observe while the squadron was assembling."

"And A obsairved," said Tam; "A obsairved the hostile enemy goin' due east. A further obsairved the squadron goin' northeast, so I just hung aroond, ma instinct tellin' me that this wee feller would return. A knew he would return, for he hadna caught anything, for awa' up A could see a wee balloon that was driftin' slowly southward."

Blackie nodded.

"Presently ma fine lad came back. He had missed it the first time and he had missed it the second time, but the third time he spotted it and off he went. A had a good peek at him through ma glasses and A saw him push out his grand little fishin'-rod, hook the cord of the balloon and hike it into the nacelle. It didna take so long to get the map and break the gas-bag. Mon, it was a grand stoont!"

Tam shook his head in admiration.

That morning the Assistant Provost Marshal of Bézierville arrested the amiable Mr. Yeldstein and impounded him and his gas-cylinders, his little balloons of gold-beater's skin and a great deal of correspondence which interested the Intelligence Department long after Mr. Yeldstein had filled the grave which willing hands had dug for him.

CHAPTER VIII

THE WOMAN IN THE STORY

Tam walked to the door of his hut and peered cautiously forth. He commanded a view of one corner of the aerodrome, but it was a corner from which Cadet William Best was not in sight, and Tam closed the door and returned to his writing-table, muttering uncomplimentary words.

He squared his shoulders to the monumental task he had set himself. Filed neatly before him in the heart of an official blue folder labeled "Corps Orders," the flaps outspread and ready to be closed at the first alarm, were some hundred quarto sheets of manuscript written in Tam's peculiar caligraphy.

The first page bore, one under the other, some five titles, all of which had been crossed out. So whatever this thrilling romance might be called eventually, it would not be, "The Terror of the Sky," or "The Birdman of Blood," or "The Crime in the Clouds," or "Looping Larry's Last Lap," nor even "The Pirate Pilot."

This was Tam's guilty secret, a secret he shared with Boy Billy Best. He was writing a book; at least he and Billy were writing it in collaboration, for if there was some uncertainty as to what the title of this "Story of Mystery and Crime" (to quote the subtitle) should be, its authorship was definitely ascribed in carefully printed characters to "Tam McTavish, R.F.C., and Cadet William Best, U. S. Army."

Tam took up his pen, dipped it slowly in the ink and wrote:

"It was a terrible moment for the brave lads of the air. What should they do? Hector felt his heart beating, his throat was filled with black rage and hate, his hands were working convulsively."

Beyond this Tam could not make Hector go. Hector was the hero who had been sent forward from the City of the Plains to make a reconnaissance. The City of the Plains (conveniently adjacent to the Mexican border) was awaiting the advent of an invading army and Hector had discovered that same army advancing through a pass in the mountains.

The scene had been laid, against Tam's better judgment, in America. Tam had suggested that it should be laid in Scotland, a suggestion which Billy had rejected with scorn.

"The Scots haven't got any enemies."

"A'm no' so sure about that," said Tam.

"Well, who would you be at war with, anyway? You haven't anybody on your borders who are likely to invade Scotland except the English."

Tam shook his head in doubt.

"There's a gey lot of tourists come to Scotland in the summer," he said, but he had agreed that his suggestion was weak. So the story became American, and Tam was reconciled to the overriding of his views by the fact that the American public would "go crazy," as said the enthusiastic Billy.

"A'm no' so sure," said Tam, "that they'll go as crazy as that. Noo, my idea is that we've got this story a' wrong. Theer's nae woman in it—"

"Woman!" scoffed Billy Best. "You're mushy, Tam! What's a woman to do with flying? For the Lord's sake!"

"Ye talk like the meenister of the wee kirk," said Tam; "'tis a wonder ye fly at a' wi' such a wind-pressure, Billy. There's nae sentiment in ye. Mon, where's the gentle-faced dauchter of the auld trapper that's been lured awa' by the deadly Choctaws? Wheer's the Pride of Minin' Camp wi' a pair o' six-shooters? Have ye ever known a story that hadn't a girlie in it?"

"This is a story," insisted the obstinate Billy," of flying, and there isn't going to be a woman in it—it'll be a novel story."

"Ye're inhuman," said Tam, but he did not press the matter.

And here he was held up and Billy, the faithless collaborator, who had sworn by all his gods, including Gee and Giminy and Gosh, that he would return at four o'clock from Amiens, had not kept his appointment.

Tam made one more attack upon Hector before he laid down his pen, but the attack was repulsed with heavy losses to Tam's confidence and, with a sigh, he folded away the manuscript and locked it in his drawer.

He made a careful search of Billy's belongings, felt in his pockets, opened his suitcase, groped under his bed, turned back his pillows and found the box of cigars that Billy had secreted, helped himself, replacing the box under his own pillow, and made his way to the mess-room.

Half a gale was blowing and the sky was filled with flying clouds, and Tam did not need to pause at the notice-board in the mess-room to read the weather report and forecast. There would be no "Wind S. W. 6 miles at 3,000 feet, light ground mists," for the barometer was still falling.

In these circumstances he expected to find the mess full and was not disappointed. The smoking-room was crowded, for such weather as this which makes flying impossible, enables airmen to pay social calls upon their fellows and adds a pleasant variety to the bridge-tables, which are inclined to become rather monotonous and stodgy when the same people play night after night.

There were no cards on the table, partly because the visitors were sitting on them and partly because there was a great discussion in progress.

Weatherby, squadron commander of the Umpty-ninth, with two rows of ribbons on his breast and only a faint suspicion of hair on his upper lip, yelled a welcome to Tam as he came in.

"Ask Tam!" he shouted—you had to shout to make yourself heard when twenty-five strategists were all offering their views at one and the same time.

Blackie looked round over his shoulder. "What do you think, Tam, about the offensive? Where is it going to be?"

"Or is it going to happen at all?" demanded Weatherby. "We've just come down from the Ypres salient. No signs of Huns there, except the usual crowd."

"How far did you go back?" demanded Blackie.

"As far as Namur. The only remarkable thing about the trip was the number of 'hates' I got. I was hated in all sorts of funny places where you never saw an Archie battery before."

"Railway junctions?" suggested somebody.

Weatherby shook his head. "No," he said, "you expect them there. On plain bits of the line where there are no villages or houses, in open fields—there was no method about it. I was quite rattled after a bit. Of course, they gave me hell at Namur, but that is understandable. But why should I get hell at Wieglehoek, which has one farm, a church and an estaminet?"

"The Huns are trying out some new Archie batteries," suggested Rolls of Weatherby's squadron.

"That hasn't answered our question," said Blackie; "is there going to be an offensive and where? What do you say, Tam?"

"A'm no' so sure," said Tam. "A was taking a peek behind the St. Quentin front on the Sabbath and A was hated verra brightly, but there was nothing strange so far as ma puir auld eyes could tell. The peaceful land was bathed in sunlight, the little bairds were singing, and a regiment of Huns was marching away from kirk, behind their band—a gay an' gallant display. As A looked doon, the sicht of these martial men in their gentle mood, retairning maybe from a heartrending sermon about the Kaiser to their warm Sunday sausage brocht a lump to ma throat. Ma first inclination was to loose a couple of trays of ammunition at them, but ma better feelings prevailed.

"'No, no, Tam,' says I, 'yer too far off and ye mayn't hit 'em. What did the government give ye bombs for?' So I dropped a couple right in the middle of 'em."

"Did they scatter?" asked Weatherby.

"They seemed a bit put oot," said Tam, "but A didn't wait, for all the Archies in the world opened up on me."

"Some people think it will be down in the Champagne." said Blackie, "against the French. Demaurier was telling me the other day that his people had spotted a concentration there."

"More likely the Aubers Ridge." said Weatherby, shaking his head; "there's a sure break-through there in the angle of the Lys and the Lawe. Besides, they've got the ridge for observation and that's a big advantage."

"What was the quietest sector all last year? Was it no' between Arras and St. Quentin? Mon, I've flown fifty miles along that line and never seen a German in the air. I took a flight down there last week and had to fight my way oot. There's more caircuses between Quéant and St. Quentin than Barnum ever heard aboot."

"But no concentrations?" asked Weatherby.

Tam shook his head.

Billy Best was waiting for Tam when the pilot returned to his room. "Where did ye get to, Billy?" demanded Tam reproachfully; "for two hours A've been wastin' ma time discussin' the strategy an' tactics o' the war when A micht ha' been followin' ma literary career. 'What would ye do,' sez the young gentleman to me, 'suppose ye was Hindenburg?' 'Change ma face,' I says. "Would ye attack frontally or sideways?" they asked, 'or would ye use strategy or tactics or a little of both?' says they. Mon, they were frichtfully struck on ma tellin' 'em, but I wouldna!"

Tam sat down to his table and jerked out the manuscript.

"'Tis a graund nicht for romance. Billy," he said, "but A'm stuck. A've got Hector in an awfu' position— listen to this:

"Hector glanced left and right an' behint him. There was no one in sicht but the hated foe. His radiator was smashed an' his intake—'"

"See here, Tam," said Billy in his shirtsleeves, with his back to his companion, "why not make Hector pancake or crash and have him rescued by a beautiful French girl who hides him, eh?" his voice was careless, so was his hand, for as he splashed water into the big enameled basin, preparatory to making his evening ablutions, certain errant drops reached Tam's neck, "or, how would it be if a mysterious triplane comes barging out of a cloud and rescues the falling hero, and it turns out that this fellow—"

"The clood or the triplane?" asked Tam politely.

"This pilot fellow, I mean, isn't a man at all, but just a peach of a French girl?"

Tam put down his pen and turned. "Billy," he said, eying the boy keenly, "what's the matter wi' ye?"

Billy blushed and rubbed his face vigorously with a towel.

"Oh, nothing," he said airily.

"Where have ye been?" asked Tam.

"Well, to be honest, Tam—I've been to see a friend of mine."

"I feared it," said Tam sadly. "What's her name and in what store in Peronne does she sairve the picture postals to the ribald soldiery?"

Billy blushed more furiously than ever.

"Oh, you know her, do you, Tam? She's just fine, that girl! Think of it! She's never been out of the battle zone—her brother was killed at Roye and her father at Verdun and she just hangs on with her mother and won't budge. They're wonderful, these Frenchwomen, pour la France, and all that sort of thing, Tam—full of grand spirit and—"

"Hark at the heathen American talking French!" said Tam addressing the roof; "'pour la France,' says he, an' it's been pourin' all the day. Billy, when ye were pourin' la France over a grocery counter did ye no' think of the girl ye left in Washin'ton, Ohio, or whatever the shire may be? Did ye no' remember the girl that stood on the quay at Phullydelphia an' watched the big ship carry ye away, her bright an' luminous eyes filled wi' tears? Did ye no' recall Maisie—"

"Maisie!" gasped Billy, recovering from the trance into which Tam's inventive genius had thrown him, "I don't know—I haven't a girl—and, anyway, I didn't sail from Philadelphia."

Tam replaced the manuscript and rose. "Billy," he said, "A'm goin' to talk to ye fer yeer good."

"Have a cigar," invited Billy hastily.

"Ye can't bribe me—unless ye've something better than the cheap trash ye keep under yeer pillow—anyway, A don't want to smoke. Billy—it's a graund idea, the descendants of George L. Washin'ton—"

"What's the L for, anyway?" growled Billy.

"Late," replied Tam calmly; "it's a graund idea for the great-grandson of George L. Wash'in'ton to wed the heiress of the McLafayette, but, Billy, we can't do it—"

"Who's talking of marrying?" grumbled the boy. "She wouldn't have me, anyway. I don't want to do anything but just look at her—God, it makes me feel good. Tam! It's like a mind bath to know that that kid has just stuck to her post—when the Boche was in Peronne, when the Somme battle was in full swing and is still carrying on."

Tam was silent. He had an instinct as delicate as a woman's and he visioned the clean splendor of the boy's mind.

"Oh, aye," he said gently, "tis a fine race, Billy, even if they do charge ye the price for butter that ye ought to pay." (Tam had taken on temporarily the post of mess caterer during the president's absence on leave and the price of local luxuries had left their mark upon him.) "But A doot if Peronne's a good place to be."

"She's all right," said Billy confidently; "she's got a big dugout behind the store and when the Boche is night bombing, she skips in there."

"A'm no' thinkin' of night bombin'," said Tam. "Billy, the Boche is gettin' ready for his big push—he'll take Peronne."

"Rats," scoffed Billy.

"Ah weel," said Tam, and that ended the discussion.

The next day was fine and Tam made a reconnaissance eastward—so far eastward that he saw....

Back he came at top speed, dodging barrage of shell and airplane, intent only upon carrying the information he had acquired to headquarters.

The British knew the worst three days before the blow fell—but three days is all too short a warning. Divisions began moving from remote corners of France, but still with caution. Reserves stood in readiness from Dunkirk to Champagne—but at any moment a change of enemy direction might be noted.

Fourteen divisions strung along a front of fifty miles, three divisions in the rear their only reserves, and, on top of it all, fog! Fog that hid the railways, the roads, the vital nodal points! Fog that tied the fuming airmen to the ground while the rumble of the guns increased to a thunderous chorus! Fog that lifted tantalizingly and sent hundreds of machines roaring upward only to come groping their way back at terrible peril to themselves. Not a fog as you understand fog—a thick wall which blots out immediate objects—but the fog which blurs all objects on the ground at a distance of a thousand feet.

Then came the night of the twentieth. Somewhere in the mist behind the horizon formed by the spires and roofs of Cambrai, behind the stark woods and the rolling hills, lay danger. The horizon itself was blurred and limited by the mists which kept the outposts straining ears and eyes for some hint of the mystery which overhangs all battle-fields on the eve of an offensive. Gunner officers in their solitary observation posts could do no more than record the hits that came within their restricted view. The telltale flash of enemy guns was hidden from them and such counter battery work as "O.Pip" could control was little.

[* Observation post.]

Save for the ceaseless clang of the opposing artilleries which had grown in intensity during the night, there was no sign of unusual activity. "O. Pip" reported strange happenings he had witnessed in the twilight; for example, he had seen German field batteries gallop up into action and unlimber. He had seen the teams gallop back again, leaving the guns stranded and apparently unattended, though he guessed that the gun crew had dug themselves in, or had taken positions near trenches which the obliging German infantry had dug for them on the previous night.

The guns were too near the enemy's front line to capture, and an inquisitive patrol of the Black Watch which went out to investigate, not this but other strange phenomena the night before, had not returned. A kilted figure lying on the German wire had been revealed through glasses, but even this told the men nothing. Fog and the night hid the feverish preparations which were going on at the back of beyond. The French and British airmen going about their desperate business, could switch their bomb releases and send their whistling charges into the black void below, could in the momentary glare of the explosion glimpse tiny transport lorries and black snakes of men threading the narrow streets of the town, or in the bursting white light of a flare, note the congestion of carriages and trucks in the railway station they were attacking, but such things indicated no more than normal activities on the part of the army.

And yet from a hundred stations and sidings, the men in field gray were pouring, knapsacks belted about with their heavy great-coats and crowned with spare boots, bombs at their belts, two days' rations of food and an iron ration in their haversacks, one hundred and fifty rounds of ammunition in their pouches, gas-masks at the "ready" and the gripping fear of the morrow in their hearts.

Storm troops, those ugly darlings of the corps, were there, lightly equipped, but well supplied with bombs. The gas corps, the flame-throwing corps and, somewhere in the background, those sinister Pomeranians whose duty it is to strip and bury the dead.

All night long the reserves were moving up, for it was the eve of "Michael's Day," the day of victory, the day of vengeance. The British line was to be pierced and turned northward, the French pushed back beyond the swampy estuary of the Somme—and then in good time and at the Germans' leisure, both enemy armies were to be destroyed.

Endless were the columns that came tramping through the night; never ceasing was the clatter and clamor of shunting trucks and rolling wheels. Von Berne's corps to the north was deploying. Lindequist's corps on his left was up to fullest strength and had a reserve division to make sure. Kuhne's, Grunert's and Stael's corps—a phalanx of gray coats accurately marshalled under Otto von Below, the newest German hero.

The Umpty-fourth stood waiting in the mist, standing by their machines—waiting, waiting—

"My God, this is awful—this mist! Do you think—do you think they'll take Peronne—but she'd have time to clear, wouldn't she, Tam—"

Tam made no reply.

Not that day nor yet the next was Peronne taken. There were days and nights of furious, frantic endeavor, when men worked and fought without sleep, when the Umpty-fourth aerodrome was shelled to a blackened heap, when day reconnaissance followed night bombing without intermission, and haggard-faced pilots hawked through the skies, sustained by the sense of the army's imminent peril.

The day after Peronne fell Blackie sent for Tam. They were occupying a new aerodrome to the west of the Amiens line and Tam had slept for six hours on the bare ground, a sleep of sheer exhaustion, when he was awakened by Blackie's summons. That great man, unshaven, chewing vigorously at the end of a cold cigar, beckoned Tam into the hut which served as his headquarters.

"A special mission for you, Tam," he said; "there's a woman in Peronne who calls herself Marie Vaupois. Her real name is Clara Geth. She was left behind in Peronne when the Germans evacuated the town, and she had collected a whole bunch of information. Our intelligence tells us that she's leaving at eleven o'clock by motor-car for Spa. I haven't time to tell you how she hoodwinked the French authorities or impersonated the daughter of a French soldier, but she kept a little picture-post-card shop."

Tam put his hand to his eyes. "Aye," he said unsteadily. "What would ye have me do, Captain Blackie, sir?"

"It's a chance in a hundred, but you may have the luck," said Blackie rapidly; "she mustn't reach Spa. She carries too much in her head for our comfort. Kill her. You can either bomb her or machine-gun her, but she's got to be killed. It's a rotten job, I know," he said clapping the other on the shoulder, "but if you look carefully over the ground, Tam, as you pass, you will see hundreds of our own fellows who are lying unburied because a woman like that has been working secretly—"

"Oh aye," said Tam.

He swung out without another word. The riggers had finished repairing his machine and she was loaded up. Soon he was zooming up into the clear skies, heading for Peronne. He fought off an attempt that was made to intercept him and a few minutes before eleven reached the north road which runs through Gouzeaucourt.

The roads were crowded with troops, but presently he saw a car speeding up one side which had been left clear and he dropped for observation and attack. The lorry Archies blazed at him. Machine guns came into action and their bullets zipped through his wings. He saw the troops break from the road to cover but the car sped on and at the back he caught a glimpse of a woman with a purple motor-veil and swooped down almost vertically, his machine gun cackling furiously.

Nothing could live under such a fire. He had one glimpse of a huddled figure in the tonneau before the car swerved into a ditch and overturned. Then he set his face for home.

He landed in the aerodrome and Billy came to meet him with a radiant face.

"Tam, Tam," he yelled, "I've had news!"

Tam's heart stood still.

"Have ye, Billy?" he said quietly.

"She got away, Tam. Nobody saw her after the Germans came in, and her house wasn't touched. Isn't that bully? Gee! I'd like to see her just for two minutes," said the boy, his eyes shining.

Tam looked down. For his part he was trying not to see her.

CHAPTER 9

"Tam," said Billy.

Tam sat at his table, his pen poised, his eyes fixed on the calendar which hung on the wall. So he had been staring for ten minutes.

"Tam."

Tam woke from his reverie with a start and, laying down his pen, turned to his companion.

"What is it, Billy?" he asked, and there was a note in his voice which was new to Billy Best.

"Did you know that the Infant Samuel brought down Gray and Mirdle to-day?"

"Ye don't say—puir lads."

Long usage to the tragedies of war flying had never dulled his sensibility. There was always the same tremor of concern in his voice whenever a good comrade passed.

"Deid," he asked, "or missing?"

"Smashed up—fell inside our lines; they'll both recover."

Tam took up his pen again and sucked the end. "The wee lad is gettin' ower bold," he said; "it's no' his habit to strafe chasers."

Billy, his hands behind his head, lay on his bed watching a spider on the ceiling. Presently: "Tam—I've fixed that interview with de Lisle—Buller says he'll come. Could you pick us up on the Amiens road— we're going out to buy some things early and could go on to de Lisle."

"Oh, aye," said Tam absently.

Another long pause.

"Tam—what's biting you?"

"Eh?"

"You've been moping all day—are you in love?"

Tam uncrossed and crossed his legs before he replied.

"Weel," he said cautiously, "A've a friend, Billy."

Billy remembered that Tam never spoke of his wife except in these terms, and sniffed, and Tam's hard face softened in a smile as tender as a woman's.

"'Tis the fashion to pretend that ye've only to be marrit to be miserable, Billy." he said. "A've kent hundreds an' hundreds of laddies like ye. 'Tis one of the illusions of youth, like the illusion that ye can win money by playin' the races or by pickin' the pea from the thimble."

He returned his gaze to the calendar and a troubled frown wrinkled his forehead.

"You bein' American an' ma—ma friend bein' American," he said, "maybe ye'll understand what A'm tellin' ye—it's a michty sacred confidence A'm gi'in' ye, Billy."

"Go ahead, Tam—have a cigar?"

"No, Billy; this is verra serious—weel, a seegair will no' make it worse—thank ye." He bit off the end of the proffered weed. "Billy, ma friend has been writin' strange letters to me. Maybe in yer abysmal ignorance o' women yer instinct will help ye to understand where ma matured reason lets me crash."

Billy ignored the challenge and allowed the slur on his judgment to pass. He knew Tam well enough to recognize in the half-whimsical, half-serious preamble a certain strained anxiety.

"A willna tell ye everything—but ye know ma friend married—well, 'twas what the young feller who does the society notes in the Scotsman calls a miss-alleeance— she marrit beneath her."

He swallowed something and Billy was silent.

"A've been verra, verra happy wi' ma friend, Billy," Tam went on slowly, "an' she writes twice a week regularly an' they're letters—Billy, they're no' mortal in their kindness."

He stopped again, still staring at the calendar, his strong hands clasping and unclasping in his perturbation.

"I got a letter this morn," he said in a low voice," 'twas sweet an' lovin', but, mon, it was sad! It was like a letter from the dyin', Billy—the letter of a dear body knockin' at Peter's Gate an' sendin' one wistfu' glance back—A canna read it to ye, but 'twas a' regrets an' hopes—would A love her memory as A loved—"

He choked and stopped and his chin went down to his breast. Presently, with an impatient sideway jerk of his head, he went on.

"It's the fear in the letter—Billy—that just sickens me—that makes ma verra soul curl up like a parched paper—God knows what it's a' aboot. Maybe she knows she's made a mistake, the puir lassie, maybe she's met some lad she kent awa' back in America—"

"And maybe she's fed up with waiting for you to go on leave, Tam," said Billy wisely; "after all, it must be six months since you went to England—"

"Scotland," murmured Tam, "though she's in England now."

"Well, go back home—you can't expect a girl to sit down and patiently wait without grouching. Now, I understand women, Tam—"

Tam was smiling now, smiling through tears. "Awa' wi' ye, ye arrogant pup!" he said in quite his old tone; "but maybe ye're right an' A'll ask leave in the morn. Noo help yersel' to one of yer ain seegairs, an' we'll have a graund talk about the Infant Samuel."

And of him they talked until the small hours, for the Infant Samuel was that phenomenon, the perfect air-fighter, and that he happened to be a German in no way detracted from the interest that was felt in him even on the civilized side of the battle-line.

Therefore did they speak of him until they slept, and met the next day, reinforced by a third redoubtable fighter, to speak of him again.

A solemn old gentleman of twenty-three—and twenty-three feels horribly old when it has killed its seventeenth man—sat at a round table in that most disreputable of estaminets (it was called most incomprehensibly "The Grand Choice" and stands on the Amiens-Arras road) and discussed the art and practise of wilful murder, the paucity of leave and the perfectly ripping qualities of Yorkshire terriers with our sober veteran of nineteen who had three or four slaughters, several attempted suicides and divers other acts of violence to his credit.

"The great thing is to keep away from stereoptyped methods, Billy," said the sage of twenty-three, whose name was Buller. "That's where so many fellows go wrong. They patent a new stunt and work it too long. Presently Fritz gets 'em taped—"

"How's that?" said Billy.

"Gets wise to 'em," translated Buller; "the counter-stunt appears one fine morning and the patent lapses, owner being too dead to renew. They are bound to cut you sooner or later," went on this cheerful youth complacently, "and likely as not you'll be brought down by a beastly Archie or shot down by a puddin' headed Prussian private. But it's your job to prevent yourself being outed in a legitimate way."

"I get you," said Billy. "Now, Tam says—"

"Oh, Tam," said Buller with respect; "well, you see, Tam is always inventing new stunts and he never tries 'em more than three times. Tam is the only man that ever brought down a Boche machine with a hand grenade, and that wants some doing, but he never tried the hand-grenade trick twice, and Tam brought down von Bruning by falling into a tail dive and shooting up, and that was never done before. Tam has done everything and still finds new things to do. I am not talking about genius—"

"Bouquets should be left with the stage-door keeper," said Billy, "don't apologize. You mean well. Tam's all right." He looked at his wrist-watch. "Are we renting a room here?" he asked politely.

"We've got another five minutes," replied Buller, consulting his own watch.

He walked to the door of the estaminet and looked down the long road and, save for an ambulance convoy moving slowly back to the base hospital, there was no one in sight. Overhead an artillery plane was moaning its mournful way to its aerodrome and at this Buller cocked a critical eye.

"The Infant missed you, anyway," he said.

"It's a low-down business shooting spotters," said Billy. "Tam and me—"

"Tam and I," corrected the veteran.

"Tam and me," said the defiant Billy, "reckon we'll lay for the Infant Samuel and rock him to sleep, yes, sir, and—there's Tam."

Tam was no more than a swift-moving cloud of dust on the long road. Presently the cloud thinned and revealed a small motor-car and Tam drew up his machine chick-a-chucking noisily.

"'Tis the best A could do," said Tam, "an' will ye be so kind, Mr. Buller, as to say nothin' that will hairt the patriotic feelin's o' ma wee friend, Billy—"

"The fellow that made that car is turning out two submarine chasers a day," said Billy, not without pride. "He's going to make thousands of one-man submarines—"

"I've heard that, but where will he get his crews?" asked the practical Mr. Buller; "you'll want pretty daring fellows for a job like that."

"What's the matter wi' the fellers who drive his cars?" asked Tam. "Mon, it wants nairve. Get in, Mr. Buller—that bit o' tin wi' the handle is the door. Hauld tight—A'm goin' to start."

You may imagine three enthusiastic Egyptologists taking long journeys to consult a fortunate fourth who had seen with his own eyes the scarab of Amen-Ra; or the pilgrimage of three astronomers to compare notes with one who has discovered in the spectrum of Nueva Aquilæ the lines of calcium; or the journeyings of zoologists to greet the traveler who, in the deeps of the Bongindanga forest, has had the good fortune to photograph an okapi. It requires an adaptable imagination to understand the object of the journey which three members of the Flying Corps were taking.

These three young men were great craftsmen, great enthusiasts and great scientists. They were slayers of men, but that was only incidental to the greater business of their days. The killing of a man merely marked the completeness of their achievement. If they could have tagged an enemy airplane with red chalk, and by such marking passed the machine and its occupants automatically from service, they would have been satisfied. They were on their way now to talk with a hero of twenty and a few odd months who could tell them ever so many things about another young gentleman they wanted to kill.

The hero lived in a big aerodrome behind the French lines (to the relief of Billy, who had rashly undertaken the duties of interpreter, he spoke excellent English), and when the three musketeers found him he was eating large slices of bread and cheese and jam and washing it down with immense drafts of vin ordinaire.

He was the French ace de Lisle, and he had a transparent little mustache and about twelve medals.

"M'sieur," said Billy valiantly, "pardon si nous dérangez—"

"Dérangons," murmured Buller; "we're plural."

"And singular too," laughed de Lisle. "Tam, Bill-ee Best and Buller, isn't it? Welcome, my aviators! What is happening on your part of the line? Bissing's circus was performing the last time I heard from you."

He seated them, energetically talking all the time.

"Weel, ye see, Mr. de Lisle," said Tam, "it's aboot the Infant Samuel we've come to see ye—"

"Ah. The Bébé! Good!" smiled de Lisle. "Yes, we know him and I have seen him. A cherub, by gar! An angel! He has been on the Champagne front for a year and a terrible fellow he has been, par-bleu! I was taken prisoner a month ago and saw him—engine failed and down I went into the Boche lines. He came down after me and I saw him. At first I thought it was a little girl when I saw him jump from his machine and come across to me. I was amazed, dumfounded; it was incredible! Blue eyes, hair like spun gold— not cut short, Boche fashion, but curly; complexion like a peach and the smile of a beneficent cupid! And polite, m'sieurs! A veritable gentleman. Saxon, of course—age about seventeen and the pride of the German army. I have tried to kill him twice since then—I escaped, as you know, on the night of my capture and I am not allowed to cross the German lines any more." He shrugged his shoulders, desolated.

"He must be a graund little feller," said Tam. "I'd love to have a crack at him. What like's his machine?"

"Fokker improved," said de Lisle; "it turns very quickly and is a devil of a climber."

"What are his stunts?" asked Billy.

"All of them," replied de Lisle promptly. "He shoots up from below, and you want to be careful about getting on his tail—he has a trick of stalling and shooting backward. He'll never give you the sun—that's certain. I've never known a man who got between him and the sun. He shoots better to the left than to the right, and the only way you'll ever get him is to zoom up at him on his blindest side—that's the right, and my faith! that infant has very good sight on the blind side, too!"

For an hour the talk ran to and fro like the shuttle of a loom, leaping from Tam to de Lisle, from de Lisle to Billy, from Buller to Tam, and presently there was woven a good piece of education in the ways and wiles of the Infant Samuel.

They went back to their quarters that afternoon with important data common to all three, but with three views on the best method of employing their knowledge.

Buller, on early patrol duty, spent the greater part of the night planning his method of attack and went up confidently.

"Wish you were in this flight, Tam," he said at parting. "I feel I'm going to meet the Infant."

"Bring me back a lock o' that golden hair," said Tam gruesomely. "Billy is makin' a collection."

Buller's prophecy was fulfilled. He met the Infant over Citie St. Augustine, north of Lens, and attacked him from below. The Infant turned and windmilled, wing over wing, and Buller, pulling clear of the disorder, exposed himself for the fraction of a second....

"Buller is down," said Blackie, coming into the mess for breakfast; "fell in our lines, poor chap."

No need to ask any further question. The "poor chap" was all the announcement that need be made.

Buller, with a puzzled smile frozen on his white face, was lying in a trench covered by an army blanket and the R. A. F. mechanics were already digging his grave.

"Pass the toast, Tam," said Billy gruffly. Tam knew just how he felt.

Later in the morning they learned that it was a veritable Infant kill. Witnesses there were in plenty and victims also. The pilot and observer of a stricken artillery bus on the Arras road had seen the fight—and had even felt its repercussion.

"They've given a circus to that Infant," telephoned the brigadier to the headquarters of the Umpty-fourth; "for the moment he's pursuing Richthofen's tactics."

Richthofen's tactics were familiar to every airman. The leader commands a dozen swift machines and the circus patrols in formation. The task of the eleven is rounding out any sky stragglers they meet to ring them round until escape is impossible. Then the leader on number twelve drops to deliver the coup de grace. It is only possible over the German lines, which means that it is always possible because it is there where the Allied airmen are to be found.

The Umpty-fourth turned out in full strength.

"Tam," yelled Billy, as he flung himself into his quarters, "there's going to be a real dog fight—why, what's the matter?"

Tam was standing by the window, his face drawn and haggard.

"It's another letter, Billy," he said huskily; "ye can see it."

Billy took the half sheet of note-paper.

There were only a few lines written in pencil:

God bless you, my boy, and help you to bear whatever trial He sends you. I am happy in a sad way, believing whatever is, is best. — V.

Billy handed the letter back without comment.

"A've asked for leave an' A'll be leavin' to-morrow forenoon," said Tam, as he folded the paper and put it in his breast pocket.

Billy had no words. His heart was aching for his comrade and he felt horribly inadequate and deficient.

They walked across the flying-ground in silence.

"So long, Tam," said Billy as he came to his machine, and Tam gripped his hand and passed on.

The fighting scouts went up one by one and maneuvered for formation. Soon they were heading for the northeast to avenge their dead. The artillery spotters saw them sail majestically to their goal, a grim and beautiful spectacle.

They were in action between Roulers and Lille—a short savage scrap with a flight of six German battle-planes—and there was a mighty rocketing and looping. The air pulsed with the incessant splutter of machine-gun fire. Eight machines fell blazing to the earth and the squadrons reformed and continued eastward, for they had annihilated their enemies.

Tam swung his machine into position, saw Billy three hundred yards away on his right rear and waved his hand. Nothing happened until Blackie signaled "Return."

They were nearing Lille when the reinforced Archie barrage split them. Tam led his flight to the right, following the course of the Lys. It was above the ruins of Armentières that the Infant struck. Six enemy machines drove toward the flight and Tam, observing the fan-shaped formation and the central chaser at a lower level, knew that this was the opportunity he sought.

He came down with one wing up to blind his adversary and brought his gun into action. The Infant came round on a quick turn and let go a burst at the higher machine. Tam stalled the scout and fell back vertically, with his undercarriage exposed to his enemy, who again swooped round, this time in a wider circle, in the hope of reaching a vulnerable place.

Tam thought he had his man. Down went his nose and straight he drove to the enemy's flank. The maneuver which followed was one of lightning swiftness. The Infant stalled, but in stalling came round so that the belly of his big machine faced the onrush—then through the floor of the nacelle he fired two deadly bursts.

Tam was unhurt, but his controls were gone and he was spinning for a fall. Like a flash the Infant zoomed up to give the death blow. And at that moment came Billy Best, a roaring rocket of spurting flame. The Infant banked too late. Billy saw a hand go up in involuntary protest, and the big chaser fell.

Tam was half-way to earth by now, but working feverishly to right his elevator. He was still working when his Spad pancaked and crashed on all fours, flinging him into a plowed field.

"Hurt?" Billy was down and supporting him. "Gee, Tam, I thought you'd borrowed your last cigar!"

Tam relieved his face of a coating of Flanders and shook his head. "Did ye get him?" he asked shakily.

Billy pointed. The wreckage of an airplane lay in the next field—and as they made their way across the plow, half a dozen soldiers were lifting from the débris its tiny pilot.

Pathetically small he looked, a mere wisp of a boy with matted golden hair that cascaded over his forehead.

He opened his eyes and smiled up at the two.

"Hard luck—yes," he whispered in English, "Can I drink?"

Billy knelt by his side and lifted his shoulders from the ground and put the nozle of a water-bottle to his lips.

"What time is it?" he asked.

It was ten minutes past one and they told him.

"Will you please tell me who you are—oh, yes—Tam and Best, that is the American who used to ram machines; you will carry a message over the lines to the Roulers aerodrome, please. Also will you write a message for my—mother—You are very kind—"

He closed his eyes drowsily.

The blood patch was spreading across his gray tunic and Tam knew the end was near.

"Tell her I was very happy—yes? I am young—but I have lived."

His smile was the smile of a child; the powder-grimed hand that lay on his breast was as delicate as a woman's.

"Bismarckstrasse 97," he murmured and then, as though in his delirium he recalled the nickname the English had given him, "Speak, Lord, for Thy servant heareth."

And so saying he died.

They saw the body put on an ambulance before the car came to carry them home and neither spoke until the aerodrome was in sight.

"Billy," said Tam solemnly, "yon was a verra guid boy."

"You bet," said Billy, chewing vigorously and looking straight ahead.

"It's an awfu' waste, this war," said Tam.

Billy turned and looked at him.

"I tell you how I figure it out, Tam," he said a little incoherently, "something better is going to grow in the place of all the good things the war has burnt. It's a weeding-out, Tam—that's how I figure it. I guess that for every soul that goes out to God there's another soul blooming—this sounds slush and I wouldn't say it to anybody but you. These fellows who die don't really die—they just fade aside and make way for the men and women who will come along the path they died to open up. Do you see, Tam—that's how I figure it."

Tam gripped the boy's arm in his and squeezed it tight.

The car drove straight to the headquarter office and Blackie bounded out to meet them.

"Thank God you're back!" he said.

Now it was not usual for Blackie to express his thanks publicly for his blessings, and Tam looked at him with interest.

"Here," said Blackie and handed the scout a field-telegraph form.

It was addressed to Tam and read:

WE HAVE A DARLING BOY, TAM—I AM SPLENDIDLY WELL. WHAT SHALL WE CALL HIM? VERA.

Tam turned his head and looked back down the long white road. An ambulance was coming briskly toward the hospital which lay beyond the aerodrome and he recognized it.

"We will call him Samuel," he said, and then the old bubbling spirit which was peculiarly his, broke through, "after Uncle Sam," he added.

Edgar Wallace – A Short Biography

Richard Horatio Edgar Wallace was born on the 1st April 1875 at 7 Ashburnham Grove, Greenwich. His mother, Mary Jane "Polly" Richards was born into an Irish Catholic family in Liverpool in 1843 and had worked in theatres, both as an actress in bit-parts and as a stagehand and usherette, until she married a Merchant Navy Captain, Joseph Richards, in 1867. He too had been born into an Irish Catholic family in Liverpool. His father had also been a Captain in the Merchant Navy, and his mother's family had a marine background. Mary was eight months pregnant with Joseph's child when he died at sea, and it was once the child had been born that she first turned to the stage, taking the stage name Polly Richards.

She joined the Marriott family theatre troupe in 1872. It was managed by Mrs. Alice Edgar, Richard Edgar, Grace Edgar, Adeline Edgar and Richard Horatio Edgar, Wallace's father. In late 1874 Mary and Richard Horatio Edgar had a brief sexual encounter at the party following a successful show, and she fell pregnant. Worried about the scandal which would ensue and fearing that she might forever lose her job at the troupe, she fabricated an obligation in Greenwich would detain her there for at least six months. She lived in a room in the boarding house on Ashburnham Grove until her son, Edgar, was born. She had already made preparations through her midwife for a couple to foster the child, and when Edgar was born the midwife presented her with Mrs Freeman. Her husband was a fishmonger at Billingsgate market and she already had ten children. She was happy to foster the child and for Polly to make frequent visits to see him in exchange for a small sum of money which Polly made from her work in the theatre troupe.

Wallace was now known as Richard Horatio Edgar Freeman, taking his father's forenames and his foster family's surname. Broadly speaking his childhood was a happy one. The Freemans looked after him lovingly and he had good friendships with his foster siblings, particularly Clara Freeman, twenty years his senior, who often looked after him as a child. After a few years Polly's finances tightened and she was no longer in a position to afford the fee she had been paying the Freemans. However, they had grown to love the young Wallace and opted to adopt him in order to keep him out of the workhouse. Polly could no longer visit him. George Freeman was keen to ensure that he had equal opportunities and did all he could to secure him an education at St. Alfege with St. Peter's, a Peckham boarding school. Despite his adoptive father's efforts, though, Wallace left the school aged twelve for truancy.

Instead he went to work and by the time he was fourteen or fifteen he had experience selling newspapers at Ludgate Circus, near Fleet Street, as a worker in a rubber factory, as a shoe shop assistant, as a milk delivery boy and as a ship's cook. He stole from the milk company which resulted in his dismissal, and in 1894 was engaged to a local girl from Deptford named Edith Anstree, though he broke this off and instead joined the Infantry. He adopted the name Edgar Wallace which he took from Lew Wallace, the author of *Ben-Hur*, and his medical record records a diminutive 33" chest and a stunted growth. his first posting was with the West Kent Regiment in South Africa in 1896, though he did not enjoy military life, arranging to be transferred to the Royal Army Medical Corps. Though this was a less strenuous job, it was also significantly less pleasant and so he again transferred to the Press Corps, which he found suited him far better.

He was in Cape Town in 1898 where he met Rudyard Kipling and was inspired to begin writing and publishing poetry and songs. His first collection of ballads, *The Mission that Failed!* and was enough of a success that in 1899 he paid his way out of the armed forces in order to turn to writing full time. His first work was as a war correspondent for Reuters who kept him in Africa to cover the Boer War, and then for the Daily Mail in 1900 and various other periodicals after that. It was while he was in South Africa that he met and married Ivy Maude Caldecott, who was 21 when they married in 1901, despite her Wesleyan missionary father's strong opposition to the union, for several reasons, one of which was that Wallace's writing was not turning quite the profit he had expected it would. *War and Other Poems* and *Writ in Barracks,* both published in 1900, had not proved as popular as his first collection. Eleanor Clare Hellier Wallace, their first child, died of meningitis in 1903 and, in rather deep debt, they returned to London. Wallace used his contacts with the Daily Mail to get work with them in London, electing to write detective novels as a means of making quick money.

Wallace met Polly, his birth mother, in 1903. He didn't remember her from his childhood as he had been too young when she became unable to visit, so it was as though they were meeting for the first time. She was sixty years old and terminally ill, living in abject poverty. She had come to Wallace seeking financial support, but he turned her away. She died in the Bradford Infirmary later that year. In 1904 he and Ivy had a son, Bryan. He was still writing and had completed his first thriller, *The Four Just Men*. Since nobody would publish it he resorted to setting up his own publishing company which he called Tallis Press and he published a serialised version of *The Four Just Men* in 1905. He received promotional assistance from the Daily Mail in which he ran a competition for entrants to guess the method of murder in the final chapter, with a prize of £1,000 for a correct guess. Although the paper's proprietor, Lord Alfred Harmsworth, refused Wallace the £1,000 prize money, Wallace persisted and went ahead with the competition, recklessly advertising on billboards and buses all over the country, hoping to expand his advertisements across the Empire. His worried colleagues at the Daily Mail managed to convince him to lower the prize money to £500, split into a first prize of £250, a second prize of £200 and a third of

£50, but with the total cost of his advertisements nearing £2,000 he would need to sell £2,500 worth of copies before he could see any profit. He was confident that this could be achieved in just three months.

Though he had remarkable enthusiasm, it became clear that his managerial skills left a lot to be desired. It soon emerged that nowhere in the competition terms and conditions had he included a clause limiting the competition to one single winner; instead, any entrant with a winning answer was entitled to their corresponding prize money. Thus, if ten entrants guessed the first prize answer, the competition was obliged to pay each entrant £250. This error was only noticed after the competition had been closed and the solution had been printed in the final installment of the novel, meaning that not only was there no opportunity to write his way out of enormous financial obligation, but the entrants who had guessed correctly would by now have read the final chapter and know they had done so. £250 was an enormous amount of money to the average Edwardian family and those entitled to it were likely to make a lot of noise if they didn't receive their money. Despite this, Wallace's fist instinct was to attempt to ignore the issue entirely, even as he discovered that he initial calculations had been dramatically over-enthusiastic and it would take nearer to two years of continuous sales to break even at the initial cost of £2,500, let alone the new figure which included every correct guesser. Compounding the problem even further was the awful realisation that as sales continued throughout the initial three month period and Wallace approached the £2,500 break-even figure, new readers were still eligible to enter and guess correctly. Though it is unknown how much he eventually owed his readers, Lord Harmsworth found himself having to loan over £5,000 in order to protect the reputation of the newspaper, since 1906 had come around and there still hadn't been a list printed of all prize-winners. It was less a charitable act than one of a man anxious that the failure would reflect ill on his own paper. Wallace filed for bankruptcy shortly thereafter and as a token gesture to his creditors sold the rights to the novel to Sir George Newnes, a publisher and editor, for £75. In the midst of this chaos though, Wallace managed to write and published *Smithy*, which would become the first of a series of *Smithy* novels.

Following this fiascos Wallace was dismissed from the Daily Mail in 1907 when inaccuracies which were found in his reporting, resulting in libel cases being brought against the paper. That year he became the first reporter to be fired from the Daily Mail and was his awful reputation prevented him from finding work at any other papers. Despite all this, though, he travelled to the Congo Free State later that year and reported on the criminal treatment of the Congolese people by King Leopold II of Belgium and the Belgian rubber companies. Up to fifteen million Congolese were killed in various atrocities, and Wallace was asked to serialise stories based on his experiences for her penny magazine *Weekly Tale-Teller*. He and Ivy had another daughter, named Patricia, in 1908. Though his new work for *Weekly Tale-Teller* was bringing in some money, their financial situation was still dire and Ivy was occasionally forced to sell off her jewellery and possessions in order to pay for food. In 1911 his Congolese stories were published in a collection called *Sanders of the River*, which quickly became a bestseller. He would publish eleven more such collections featuring a total of 102 stories of adventure and tribal life set on the river Congo.

From 1908 he started to enjoy a revival of both his success and his reputation. The majority of his initial writing he sold outright in order to make money as quickly as possible and placate his creditors in the United Kingdom and South Africa, but as his success saw the reestablishment of his reputation he began to find work once again as a journalist, beginning in horse racing for the *Week-End*, the *Evening News* and then as an editor for the *Week-End Racing Supplement*. Following this success he started his own racing papers, *Bibury's* and *R. E. Walton's Weekly*, eventually buying his own racehorses and losing thousands gambling. His success was insufficient to support his newly extravagant lifestyle and his marriage began to fail in the light of his financial irresponsibility. He and Ivy had their last child together,

Michael Blair Wallace, in 1916, and she filed for divorce in 1918 moving to Tunbridge Wells with her children.

Wallace began to fall for his secretary Ethel Violet King and they married in 1921, having a child, Penelope Wallace, in 1923, who would herself go on to become a successful crime writer. Wallace now began to take his career as a fiction writer more seriously, signing with Hodder and Stoughton in 1921. He now began to organize his contracts more carefully, arranging for royalties and properly organized promotions, run by people more business-minded than himself. He was marketed as the 'King of Thrillers' and they gave him the trademark image of a trilby, a cigarette holder and a yellow Rolls Royce. He was truly prolific, capable not only of producing a 70,000 word novel in three days but of doing three novels in a row in such a manner. His publishers signed off on almost everything he wrote as soon as he turned it in, estimating that by 1928 one in four books being read at any time was written by Wallace, for alongside his famous thrillers he wrote variously in other genres, including but not limited to science fiction, non-fiction accounts of WWI which amounted to ten volumes and screen plays. Eventually he would reach the remarkable total of 170 novels, 18 stage plays and 957 short stories.

Wallace became chairman of the Press Club which to this day holds an annual Edgar Wallace Award, rewarding 'excellence in writing'. In 1923 he broadcasted a report on the Epsom Derby horse race for the British Broadcasting Company, making him the first ever radio sports correspondent. His ex-wife Ivy had suffered from breast cancer between 1923-1924, and it eventually killed her in 1926 despite a successful operation to remove a tumour the year before. He wrote the essay "The Canker in our Midst" in 1926 which dealt, aggressively and controversially, with the problem of paedophilia in show business, describing how children were unwittingly left open to sexual abuse, and linking paedophilia with homosexuality. Its tone has been described as "intolerant, blustering, kick-the-blighters-down-the-stairs". He was appointed chairman of the British Lion Film Corporation on the back of the success of *The Ringer* and on the agreement that he give British Lion first choice on all his future work. This contract gave him an annual salary and a large amount of stock with the company, along with a stipend on all British Lion production of his work and 10% of their annual profits. This extraordinary contract gave him annual earnings by 1929 of almost £50,000, or almost £2 million in 2014.

He now became an active figure in politics, entering the 1931 general election as a Liberal contestant in Blackpool, rejecting the current government in favour of free trade. He lost the election by over 33,000 votes and went to America in late 1931, once again deeply in debt after buying the *Sunday News* which closed six months later. In America he quickly found work as a script doctor for RKO Pictures, enjoying early success with the 1932 adaptation of *The Hound of the Baskervilles*. This success, along with that of the play *The Green Pack*, established his reputation in America and he was able to see his own work adapted for film, beginning with *The Four Just Men*. His most successful theatrical work, *On The Spot*, which explores the life of Al Capone, has been described as "arguably, in construction, dialogue, action, plot and resolution, still one of the finest and purest of 20th-century melodramas". These successes led to his assignation on RKO's "gorilla picture" which would become famous as King Kong in 1933.

He worked on the first draft though he was beginning to experience severe headaches which brought about a diagnosis of diabetes. Despite taking medication to address his condition, it deteriorated in a matter of days. His wife booked him passage home but soon heard that he had entered a coma and died of his condition and double pneumonia on the 7th of February 1932 in North Maple Drive, Beverly Hills. In his honour the bell at St. Bride's church on Fleet Street tolled for the duration of the morning while the flags flew at half-mast. He was buried near his home in England at Chalklands, Bourne End, in Buckinghamshire. Once again, at the time of his death he was in severe debt, mostly to racing bookkeepers, though these debts were settled within two years thanks to the enormous royalties his estate continued to receive from his contracts. His writing has been translated into 29 languages, and is considered one of the most important bodies of Colonial writing.

Edgar Wallace – A Concise Bibliography

African Novels
Sanders of the River (1911)
The People of the River (1911)
The River of Stars (1913)
Bosambo of the River (1914)
Bones (1915)
The Keepers of the King's Peace (1917)
Lieutenant Bones (1918)
Bones in London (1921)
Sandi the Kingmaker (1922)
Bones of the River (1923)
Sanders (1926)
Again Sanders (1928)

Four Just Men (Series)
The Four Just Men (1905)
The Council of Justice (1908)
The Just Men of Cordova (1917)
The Law of the Four Just Men (US title: Again the Three Just Men) (1921)
The Three Just Men (1926)
Again the Three Just Men (US title: The Law of the Three Just Men) (1929) a.k.a. Again the Three

Mr. J. G. Reeder (Series)
Room 13 (1924)
The Mind of Mr. J. G. Reeder (US title: The Murder Book of Mr. J. G. Reeder) (1925)
Terror Keep (1927)
Red Aces (1929)[27]
The Guv'nor and Other Short Stories (US title: Mr. Reeder Returns) (1932)

Detective Sgt. (Inspector) Elk series
The Nine Bears or The Other Man or The Cheaters (1910)
revised as Silinski - Master Criminal (1930)
The Fellowship of the Frog (1925)
The Joker or The Colossus (1926)
The Twister (1928)
The India-Rubber Men (1929)
White Face (1930)

Educated Evans (Series)
Educated Evans (1924)
More Educated Evans (1926)

Good Evans (1927)

Smithy (Series)
Smithy (1905)
Smithy Abroad (1909)
Smithy and The Hun (1915)
Nobby or Smithy's Friend Nobby (1916)

Crime Novels
Angel Esquire (1908)
The Fourth Plague or Red Hand (1913)
Grey Timothy or Pallard the Punter (1913)
The Man Who Bought London (1915)
The Melody of Death (1915)
A Debt Discharged (1916)
The Tomb of T'Sin (1916)
The Secret House (1917)
The Clue of the Twisted Candle (1918)
Down under Donovan (1918)
The Man Who Knew (1918)
The Strange Lapses of Larry Loman (1918)
The Green Rust (1919)
Kate Plus Ten (1919)
The Daffodil Mystery or The Daffodil Murder (1920)
Jack O'Judgment (1920)
The Angel of Terror or The Destroying Angel (1922)
The Crimson Circle (1922)
Mr. Justice Maxwell or Take-A-Chance Anderson(1922)
The Valley of Ghosts (1922)
Captains of Souls (1923)
The Clue of the New Pin (1923)
The Green Archer (1923)
The Missing Million (1923)
The Dark Eyes of London or The Croakers (1924)
Double Dan or Diana of Kara-Kara (US Title) (1924)
The Face in the Night or The Diamond Men or The Ragged Princess (1924)
The Sinister Man (1924)
The Three Oak Mystery (1924)
The Blue Hand or Beyond Recall (1925)
The Daughters of the Night (1925)
The Gaunt Stranger or Police Work (1925) revised as The Ringer (1926)
A King by Night (1925)
The Strange Countess (1925)
The Avenger or The Hairy Arm (1926)
'The Black Abbot (1926)
The Day of Uniting (1926)
The Door with Seven Locks (1926)
The Man from Morocco or Souls In Shadows or The Black (US Title) (1926)

The Million Dollar Story (1926)
The Northing Tramp or The Tramp (1926)
Penelope of the Polyantha (1926)
The Square Emerald or The Woman (1926)
The Terrible People or The Gallows' Hand (1926)
We Shall See! or The Gaol-Breakers (US Title) (1926)
The Yellow Snake or The Black Tenth (1926)
Big Foot (1927)
The Feathered Serpent or Inspector Wade or Inspector Wade and the Feathered Serpent (1927)
Flat 2 (1927)
The Forger or The Counterfeiter (1927)
Terror Keep (1927)
The Hand of Power or The Proud Sons of Ragusa (1927)
The Man Who Was Nobody (1927)
Number Six (1927)
The Squeaker or The Sign of the Leopard or The Squealer (US Title) (1927)
The Traitor's Gate (1927)
The Double (1928)
The Flying Squad (1928)
The Gunner or Gunman's Bluff (US Title) (1928)
Four Square Jane or The Fourth Square (1929)
The Golden Hades or Stamped In Gold or The Sinister Yellow Sign (1929)
The Green Ribbon (1929)
The Calendar (1930)
The Clue of the Silver Key or The Silver Key (1930)
The Lady of Ascot (1930)
The Devil Man or Sinister Street or Silver Steel
or The Life and Death of Charles Peace (1931)
The Man at the Carlton or The Mystery of Mary Grier (1931)
The Coat of Arms or The Arranways Mystery (1931)
On the Spot: Violence and Murder in Chicago (1931)
When the Gangs Came to London or Scotland Yard's Yankee Dick
or The Gangsters Come To London (1932)
The Frightened Lady or The Case of the Frightened Lady or Criminal At Large (1933)
The Green Pack (1933)
The Man Who Changed His Name (1935)
The Mouthpiece (1935)
Smoky Cell (1935)
The Table (1936)
Sanctuary Island (1936)

Other Novels
Captain Tatham of Tatham Island or Eve's Island or The Island of Galloping Gold (1909)
The Duke in the Suburbs (1909)
Private Selby (1912)
"1925" - The Story of a Fatal Peace (1915)
Those Folk of Bulboro (1918)
The Book of all Power (1921)

Flying Fifty-five (1922)
The Books of Bart (1923)
Barbara on Her Own (1926)

Poetry Collections
The Mission That Failed (1898)
War and Other Poems (1900)
Writ In Barracks (1900)

Non-Fiction
Unofficial Despatches of the Anglo-Boer War (1901)
Famous Scottish Regiments (1914)
Field Marshal Sir John French (1914)
Heroes All: Gallant Deeds of the War (1914)
The Standard History of the War – Volumes 1 – 4 (1914)
Kitchener's Army and the Territorial Forces:
The Full Story of a Great Achievement (1915)
Vol. 2-4. War of the Nations (1915)
Vol. 5-7. War of the Nations (1916)
Vol. 8-9. War of the Nations (1917)
Famous Men and Battles of the British Empire (1917)
Tam of the Scouts (1918)
The Real Shell-Man: The Story of Chetwynd of Chilwell (1919)
People or Edgar Wallace by Himself(1926)
The Trial of Patrick Herbert Mahon (1928)
My Hollywood Diary (1932)

Screenplays
King Kong (1932, first draft of original screenplay, 110 pages) While the script was not used in its entirety, much of it was retained for the final screenplay.
The Hound of the Baskervilles (1932, British film)
The Squeaker (1930, British film)
Prince Gabby (1929, British film)
Mark of the Frog (1928, American film)
The Valley of Ghosts (192

Short Story Collections
The Admirable Carfew (1914)
The Adventure of Heine (1917)
Tam O' the Scouts (1918)
The Fighting Scouts (1919)
Chick (1923)
The Black Avons (1925)
The Brigand (1927)
The Mixer (1927)
This England (1927)
The Orator (1928)
The Thief in the Night (1928)

Elegant Edward (1928)
The Lone House Mystery and Other Stories (1929)
The Governor of Chi-Foo (1929)
Again the Ringer The Ringer Returns (US Title) (1929)
The Big Four or Crooks of Society (1929)
The Black or Blackmailers I Have Foiled (1929)
The Cat-Burglar (1929)
Circumstantial Evidence (1929)
Fighting Snub Reilly (1929)
For Information Received (1929)
Forty-Eight Short Stories (1929)
Planetoid 127 and The Sweizer Pump (1929)
The Ghost of Down Hill & The Queen of Sheba's Belt (1929)
The Iron Grip (1929)
The Lady of Little Hell (1929)
The Little Green Man (1929)
The Prison-Breakers (1929)
The Reporter (1929)
Killer Kay (1930)
Mrs William Jones and Bill (1930)
Forty Eight Short-Stories (1930)
The Stretelli Case and Other Mystery Stories (1930)
The Terror (1930)
The Lady Called Nita (1930)
Sergeant Sir Peter or Sergeant Dunn, C.I.D. (1932)
The Scotland Yard Book of Edgar Wallace (1932)
The Steward (1932)
Nig-Nog and other humorous stories (1934)
The Last Adventure (1934)
The Woman From the East (1934) Co-written By Robert George Curtis
The Edgar Wallace Reader of Mystery and Adventure (1943)
The Undisclosed Client (1963)

Other
King Kong, with Draycott M. Dell, (1933), 28 October 1933 Cinema Weekly

Plays
An African Millionaire (1904)
The Forest of Happy Dreams (1910)
Dolly Cutting Herself (1911)
The Manager's Dream (1914)
M'Lady (1921)
Double Dan (1926)
The Mystery of room 45 (1926)
A Perfect Gentleman (1927)
The Terror (1927)
Traitors Gate (1927)
The Lad (1928)

The Man Who Changed His Name (1928)
The Squeaker (1928)
The Calendar (1929)
Persons Unknown (1929)
The Ringer (1929)
The Mouthpiece (1930)
On the Spot (1930)
Smoky Cell (1930)
The Squeaker (1930)
To Oblige A Lady (1930)
The Case of the Frightened Lady (1931)
The Old Man (1931)
The Green Pack (1932)
The Table (1932)